TAINTED IDENTITY II

CANDICE Y. DOTSON

TAINTED IDENTITY II

ACKNOWLEDGMENTS

First and foremost, praises and blessings to the Most High for making this possible. Without God's grace and mercy, we would not exist.

Secondly, to my best friend, spouse, and spiritual guide, thank you for believing, supporting, and allowing God's gift to take on its form. I love you!

"I can do all things through Christ, which strengthened me."
Phil 4:13

To all my family and friends near and far, thank you for your kind words, encouraging words and prayers. I'm profoundly grateful.

If any of you lack wisdom, let him ask of God, that giveth to all men liberally, and upbraided not; and it shall be given him.
James 1:5

I dedicate this novel to my darling daughter Kiara. May the Lord guide you thru his enlightenment thru every circumstance. Put your trust in him.

Create in me a clean heart, O God; and renew a right spirit within me.
Psalm 51:10

And last but certainly not least, thank you is not enough to express my appreciation to my readers. Blessings to you and thanksgiving to yours for taking this journey with my family and me.

Love,

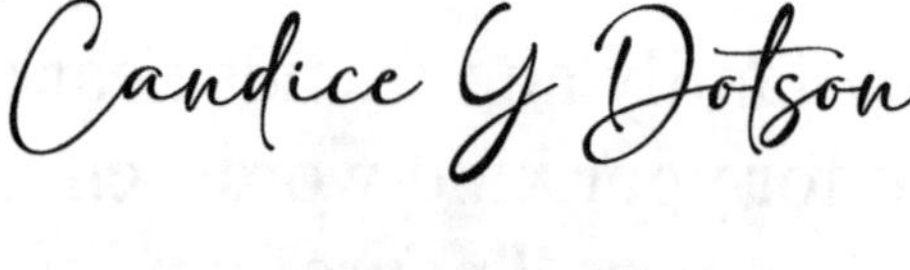

TABLE OF CONTENTS

PROLOGUE

"Get your hands off me! Stop it!"

"Oh, c'mon Marissa, I already know how you get down."

"No, I don't, plus you said we were just going to talk Lewis."

I was in a situation that was all too familiar. Do boys feel they can take what they want from you? I have feelings, emotions; I'm a human-being dammit. I met Lewis my sophomore year in high school, and though he was a nice guy, charming, good looking and all the girls wanted him, little did I know he was just like any other guy, out for one thing. Sex. Today, he was determined to have it by any means.

"So, you saying you didn't screw 'ol boy next door?" he asked skeptically.

I did lose my virginity to James, but how dare he feel that that would make me obligated to give myself to him. James was my first, and as far as I was concerned, until he gets over this Leah crush, he was, my only. "That's my business, and that doesn't make me open for business, I love James," I said

"Bullshit! All yall hoes the same." He sat back in his seat with a wave of his hand as if he's heard that before.

We were sitting in his car parked by the playground, where Leah and I had our disagreements daily during recess. I met him there because I did not want him to know where I lived, but it appears he was already aware. I became uncomfortable, and since he was displaying to me how grimy he was, I already knew I had to get out of there without setting him off.

"You know Lewis, it's getting late, and this is not going to work." I quickly opened the car door to get out, but he grabbed me by my shoulder, pulling me back into the car. "Let go of me!" I demanded. "Are you crazy?" I tried to pull away, but he had a firm grip on me.

I could feel his fingers digging into my collar bone. Before I knew it, he had maneuvered over to my side of the car, and he was on top of me. He pulled the lever to let the seat back so quickly; I didn't have a chance to catch myself. He must have done this before. It seemed all too easy for him.

"You gonna give it up today." He began to pin my arms above my head.

"STOP, STOP LEWIS! PLEASE!" I begged. I kicked and scratch as much as I could until he put his hand around my neck. I could not breathe. Fear began to fill me from the inside out, and I began to cry. He ripped my underwear and began to penetrate his penis inside me. I screamed as loud as I could. "STOP, LEWIS! WHY?"

He continued to penetrate, rapping me. Even though I was in fear of my life, I still fought. I fought because I was not going to become a victim once again by the hands of some egotistical, insecure male that could not take no for an answer. He looked frustrated and fed up with my fighting.

"Shut-up!"

I scratched and punched him so much he couldn't penetrate the way he wanted; I am sure. In his moment of weakness, I made a fist and punched him repeatedly in his face and as hard as I could. He began to maneuver back to the driver's side of the car to avoid my blows. I had gone insane, using everything in my power and strength to fight hard with each strike, my fist connected with the side of his jaw.

"Chill out!" he shouted. I continued to throw punches. I was so angry that all of my hurt from James' mistreatment of me, my Dad's abuse toward my mother and me, my uncles trying to feel me up every chance they got; I took all that emotion to beat and defeat Lewis' ass. "Marissa, calm down." I was hitting the side of his head like a piñata.

"Fuck you!" I yelled so loud my throat started to feel sore.

Lewis opened his door on the driver's side and leaned out to dodge my blows. Once I saw he had a footing on the ground, I opened my side of the door, jumped out, and ran. I ran all the way home. The adrenaline that was running through my body had me feeling like I was flying. With tears running down my face and wailing uncontrollably, I had run so fast that I didn't realize I had run past my house. When I finally got back to my house, I felt better, but then I remembered he already knew where I lived.

What if he comes looking for me? I thought.

I hurried inside and to my room so that my father would not see me. After stripping down everything I had on my body off, I got in the shower. Until I thought my skin was going to peel and bleed, I scrubbed and scrubbed. His scent and the throbbing motion of when his penis penetrated me was still alive, and I wanted it off my body. I sat down in the shower and cried until I had nothing left in me. My tears refused to flow and represent my sorrow. It was a surreal moment, and I felt stuck in time as I stared motionless at the shower drain. I allowed the water from the shower to represent my tears of pain, and hopefully, it could also cleanse me of the same.

CHAPTER 1

"Babe, can you go to the pharmacy now?" I can feel the pain from the surgery starting to worsen with each breath I took. It had only been four days since I gave birth to our son, Nathan Jr. The medication I received in the hospital was starting to wear off, and I could feel the throbbing pain from the cesarean.

"I'm trying to get this crib up first, Marissa." He looked annoyed and was not in the mood to stop what he was doing. It did not make sense to me. I needed my medicine for the pain; the crib could wait. In my opinion, my husband's priorities can be out of order, but what could I do. I was terrified of becoming a mother, and I had planned on being up all night watching him like a guy prowls a girl with a big behind. This little bundle of heaven and I were going to be sleeping side by side.

"Yes, I understand that, Nate. It's just that my pain is starting to get worse." I tried to explain. I wish he would just get the medicine, as I requested. The pain was starting to kick my butt. I had held out long enough before saying something because I knew he would go back and forth with me. His attitude toward me had been like this since I got pregnant. It seems as if I don't have a say. "Mmm." I moaned a little as I felt like my uterus had plummeted out of my ass.

Nathan fiddled with the crib for about another eight to ten minutes and finally got up to get the pain relievers. He picked up his wallet and keys and walked over by my bedside, where I was barely holding on, I was in so much pain. "Alright, I'll be back as quick as I can." I did not say anything. I was still a little pissed about him not going to get the medicine like I asked before he started on the crib.

"Do me a favor before you go," I felt like I was having contractions over again. While trying to sit up, I took a deep breath to ease the pain. "Plug up that heating pad and bring it to me so I can place it on my stomach to ease the pain, please."

Nathan did as I asked. He placed the pad on my stomach and rubbed my head. "I'll be back." I looked upon his face and took deep breaths to get through the contraction-like pain I was feeling.

"Okay." He kissed me on my forehead and left out toward the bedroom door.

Nathan Jr was sleeping on the other side of the bed surrounded by a mini fort, wrapped like a burrito you get on a taqueria truck. My mother showed me this trick when she came to visit. I know it sounds wild, but when I watched her do it, that's the first thing that came to mind. I guess I was hungry after being on a liquid diet for the past few days.

I laid there gazing at my son as the light reflected from the window upon his caramel face. He was sound to sleep and looked so peaceful. The heat from the pad was soothing, and I began to relax. My emotions started to form, and the reality was that I could not believe I was a mother. There was someone else depending on me, someone that would be looking up to me and eventually inquiring me for answers to their problems. He would look for us to keep him out of harm's way and have a childhood that the common boy would dream and want. I wondered if my parents had these exact thoughts. All I know is, I wanted to give him the best life that I could, with God's help.

My childhood seemed to be lacking that type of love. But weirdly, it taught me about love and what that word means. From what I witnessed growing up with my Dad, *his* word was bond:

"MARISSA!" my Dad yelled my name and scared me so that I got butterflies in my stomach. I got so nervous I had to go to the bathroom now. He must have found something wrong in the house. Everything had to be his way. I felt like I was on a plantation.

James Orville was a "god-fearing," dictator type. I am not saying that my father did not have a soft side at times, but they were few instead of many. My mother left because of my Dad's overbearing ways; I was seven. He wouldn't allow her to take me or see me until one day; he softened his heart enough for my mother to start getting me every other weekend. My mother was like a savior. I would love it when she would pick me up on the weekends. It was not all fun and games, she had her rules as well, but it allowed me to take the break I needed from my Dad and his in-home boot camp.

"Yes, sir." I tried to walk as fast as I could, so I would not have to hear how slow I was.

"Why are these dishes still dirty?" he asked, holding a plate in his hand.

"I cleaned it, I thought." I tried to explain nervously.

"You thought?" he tossed the plate back on the counter at me, but it slipped off and fell on the floor and shattered. "Clean it up and clean the rest of these dishes." I looked around; every dish was out of the cupboards, sitting on the counters for me to wash. "That'll teach you to do the damn dishes half-ass. What kind of husband would

want you if you can't even wash a dish, huh?" I could not wait until I could hear my Mom knocking on the door to my rescue.

When it's time for my mother to come and get me on the weekend, my father would get in this cranky mood and would take it out on me. One time he grabbed my arm and pinned me on the wall over forgetting to cut the light off in the bathroom. I told my mother, and let's just say I have not had any incidents like that again.

My Dad was an army veteran, and sometimes the effect of serving can bring out another side of him. His last duty station was at Fort Polk before he retired or was let out or something, then we moved here to Shreveport, LA, from Leesville, LA. My Dad can be the sweetest person in the world with a vivid sense of humor, and then the next become this overbearing tyrant that cannot be satisfied to save his own life.

[KNOCK, KNOCK, KNOCK]

My heart jumped, with excitement and nervousness at the same time. I know how evil my Dad can be. He will find any excuse not to let me go with my Mom, and these dishes may be just the thing. I tried eavesdropping as much as I could to listen to the conversation my Dad and Mom were having at the door. The next thing I heard was, "Let me in here, James." My mother forced her way through the door and my Dad toward the kitchen where I was. My mother was not the type to be 'ran over.' She demanded respect because she gave respect, but when it came to me, she didn't care what my father felt or what his reasonings' were for any of his actions.

I was drying the last dish when my mother walked into the kitchen. "Hey, Mom!" She hugged me as if she had just won the lottery or something. "Momma, you're crushing me." She finally let me go and took my face into her hands.

"How are you, ready to go?" she smiled and kissed my forehead. She looked back at my father, who was standing there as if he was

a chaperone with a sharp eye. "Put that stupid plate down and go get your stuff."

"Okay." I did as my mother told me and ran to my room. As I was gathering my things, I can hear my Mom and Dad going at it, as usual. There was never a dull moment between them. I did not care; I just wanted to get out of there as fast as I could. "I'm ready!" I interrupted my parents in the middle of them arguing. They were going at it so much that they didn't notice that I walked into the room, standing there absorbing each insult that they could think of to hurt one another.

My Mom stopped talking to my Dad and grabbed my hand. "C'mon Marissa. We don't need this." My Mom and I started to walk toward the door, and it felt as if I was not coming back. I'm not sure what gave me that feeling, but it came over me and warmed me like a towel fresh out of the dryer.

"You better be back here Sunday Jean, I mean it." My Dad said to my Mom. He stood

looking out the door as we walked down the steps, with his hands on his hips. As I was looking back, his face took on another form. I don't think he believed that Mom would bring me back.

Momma didn't break stride as we arrived at her car, parked on the side of the street. We got in the car and buckled up. Momma looked at me from the rear-view mirror and smiled.
"You ready sugar plum?" I shook my head in agreement. "Let's roll." The car pulled off from the curb, and a moment of euphoria filled my entire body. It was like I was an Israelite on the day that Pharaoh finally let them go.

CHAPTER 2

"Why is she calling you?" I asked Nathan. I tried to remain as calm as possible and brace myself for the obvious.

"Babe, nothing is going on. I just chatted with her once about..." he paused as if he wasn't sure if he should continue.

"About?" I became annoyed by his relaxed attitude toward the situation.

"It's just been a lot of pressure on me, and it's been hard talking to you. She is a psychiatrist, you know." I know he didn't try to use that as an excuse for him talking to an old girlfriend. I understand it was high school, but why open that door.

"What do you mean, 'hard talking to me'?" I asked.

"Look, I've known Denise since we were teenagers. I cannot just throw that friendship out the door. Now I can understand how this may come off, but that's the truth." He knelt beside the bed, where I was sitting breastfeeding the baby. "I only talked to her once, she even billed me, as you can see."

I didn't know what to believe. I was looking at the bill that prompted the call from her office. Nathan had missed a payment by mistake. Of all people he had to go to, Denise? "There was no other person you could have had a session with?" I asked with an eye roll.

"I just felt comfortable discussing my issues better with her," He said.

"Better with her?"

"No, not like that. Please don't." Nathan sat on the edge of the bed. "As a professional, Marissa."

"Well, what was so hard to talk to me about?" My face frowned up now because of the insult that was slapped in my face.

"About being afraid of being a father, Marissa." Reluctantly he revealed what I had always suspected.

"You could have told me, Nathan." I never heard Nathan say he's afraid of anything. He walks around like everything is all together in his mind. He is the bull-headed type on the outside but sweet as raw honey on the inside.

"No. I couldn't." Nate looked at me with a stern face. "I don't want you to feel like you're with someone that can't handle things."

My mother said those same words to me, the day she took me from my Dad, and I stayed with her from then on, and I started to go back and forth to my Dad's instead. My mother got the courts to say I didn't have to stay with him anymore.

I loved going to my moms' place. It would get prettier each time I would visit. Mom lived in what you call a townhome. I loved running up and down the stairs going in and out of my room. The first night, I walked in, and it was like a breath of fresh air. I turned around and hugged my Mom tightly, like a kid who got what they wanted on Christmas day:

"Yep, you're home." She bent over and held me by my shoulders and looked me directly in my face. "You're not going back there, so don't worry about that, ok?"

I shook my head, "Ok."

I am not sure what was going on between my Mom and Dad, but all I could do was just trust what my Mom was saying to me. She began to walk toward the kitchen area down the hall. When you first came in, to the right, was a big dining table. It wasn't a lot in the room, but it still looked very classy, I guess less can be better. To my left, she had a living room that looked like it should have been in a showroom. It seemed fancy, well to me. My Mom had a unique type of taste, eclectic. Everything was abstract, in my opinion, as if she didn't care what you thought. She wasn't afraid to be who she was, unapologetically.

"C'mon Marissa, you want something to eat?" my mother called to me.

I began to walk down the hallway toward the kitchen. Mom had a lot of pictures and paintings on the wall. There were quite a few of me. I turned to my right, and my Mom was in the kitchen looking in the refrigerator. She had a lot of vegetables; milk and fruit were on the counter. The other living room area, where the television was on, was beautiful and filled with colors of blue, white, and oak; eclectic furniture and floral pieces created an inviting invisible aroma. It reminded me of a picture of a Japanese home I saw in this magazine once. The natural light from the tall windows leading out to the outside patio gave it a serene feel.

Yes, I'm starving." I replied with desperation in my voice

"Figures." She said as if she had a negative thought as she rolled her eyes, looking up from her refrigerator search. "Uh, I can make a Tomato Pesto Chicken dish, how's that sound?" she asked, looking over the refrigerator door at me. I didn't care what she cooked, as long as it was fast. I was starving. "It'll take about thirty minutes or less, enough time for you to go upstairs, unpack, and wash up." She said, pointing to the bags that she brought in. I had my backpack on still and another small bag I was carrying in my hand.

"Yes, ma'am."

I went upstairs, looked around my room, and saw it was decorated nicely too, with colors of pink and cream. It looked like a three-dimensional painting of a rose garden. I unpacked my things like I do every other weekend, but this time it seemed permanent. I ran a bath and washed up for dinner. By the time I came back downstairs, I could smell the glorious aroma from the kitchen. My mouth began to water. I had to lick my lips because I know my Mom saw some spit drop off the side of my mouth when she placed the bowl of pasta and chicken in front of me. We said grace, and I dived in. It was so good; I didn't know how loud I was smacking.

"Slow down, girl." my Mom laughed but was severe at the same time.

"Oh, I'm sorry. It's good." I complimented to take the feeling of embarrassment away.

"Well, thank you." My mother was a nice person but no pushover. She was for what was fair and just. She led you in the right direction but with love. Her sincerity and grace made me feel safe.

"Marissa?"

"Yes, momma?" I said while finishing up the last bite of pasta I had. I was feeling a little disappointed and wanted to ask for seconds, but I didn't want to seem greedy.

"I know it's a lot of things that are going on between your daddy and me that you may

not understand, but I want you to know that I am capable of being the mother you need. So, whatever life brings us from here on out, I want you to know that we can handle anything that comes our way. I love you, Marissa."

"Love you too, momma; I know you can." Still chewing on my last bite. She looked at me with a sense of relief and squeezed my hand. I think she needed me to believe in her, and I did.

CHAPTER 3

It's been about six months since Nathan and I made love. Our work schedules restrict us to spend more quality time together. Working the early shift at the hospital and Nathan working as the night chef a few nights a week, almost sixteen-hours on the weekend, sometimes, it becomes challenging to make time. He and another friend of his he met in culinary school opened a restaurant. I was so proud of him, but sometimes I resent the decision that we agreed for him to take this significant step in his career, especially with junior being so young.

"Don't worry about it, Kevin is opening up for me." He said as he kissed the back of my neck and up to my ear.

I can feel the heat of his breath, warming my spine. The rhythm of his tongue against my skin had let me know he was not going to take no for an answer. The weekends were a little easier for me to breastfeed, and I had just laid the baby down after feeding him. I hated pumping milk during the workweek so, I tried to refrain from that on the weekend. It seemed better for the baby to latch on to the breast than to pump.

"You're going to wake the baby, Nate." I tried to deflect his attention because I was exhausted from working and trying to breastfeed a baby. I understood it had been a while, and I couldn't blame him for trying.

"We won't if you would put him in his room and not in here with you all the time. Its time, babe." Nathan walked over to his side of the bed and started to unbutton his shirt. I don't know what it was about him, but he was the sexiest man I have ever seen. He got in the bed and leaned back. "Go put him in the crib and come back, please."

"Nathan?"

"Am I not your husband? Am I not your husband?" He would always pull this stunt when he wants to get what he wants from me.

"Yes, you are dear." I teased.

"Well, alright, then." I rolled my eyes a little as I turned to pick up the baby and headed toward the door. "I'll be here." He said as he leaned back and put his hands behind his head, looking at me with that irresistible smile of his.

I went and put Nate Jr in his crib, brushed his head gently with my hand, and stood over his crib a while before leaving him. It was hard for me to just leave him in the room by himself, but Nathan was right; it was time to let go. I placed the baby monitors on that we had gotten from the baby shower on the dresser; one in our room and the other in the baby's room.

As I entered back into the room, Nate was out of the bed, now pulling down his pants, revealing the only stick that I've learned to drive, thanks to him. Nate was great in bed, and I found myself yearning for him inside me when I'm not around him. I thought James loved me the right way, and then I met Nate. It made me ask myself why I wasted my time on that jackass.

I remember it like yesterday when I was at my Dad's house visiting. It was the weekend I lost my virginity to James Detrick:

"Is somebody out there?" a lady called out. That was the neighborhood gossip being nosey as usual.

"Shit, shit, help me up!" James said. I grabbed his arms while he hopped through the window.

"Oh, Jes-! Hold on a minute. Ugh!" He sat on the floor under the window while I closed it slowly and quietly.

"Okay, get down." I looked through the window to peek and see if our neighbor was outside. "She's gone." That nosey bat was always lurking. "Now, what do you want?" I asked.

I was still fuming from our altercation earlier. He can be a real jerk sometimes, but

I thought he was cute. James had a confident, laid-back personality I liked but only for so long.

"Marissa, I'm sorry about earlier," he got up from the floor. "I didn't mean to insinuate that, well, I didn't mean to come off disrespectful."

"So, you come and wake me up in the middle of the night to say that?" I asked skeptically, especially since his eyes could not stop roaming up and down at me.

"Yes, you seemed upset, and that's the last thing I want. C'mon Marissa; we've known each other for a long time, I can't be as bad as I seem to be. I do care." he said. He did sound sincere, so maybe I judged before really getting to know him.

"Well, I guess. Thanks, James" I readjusted my robe and folded my arms. I do this when I start to feel awkward or when someone compliments me. I have had self-image issues for as long as I can remember.
"What?" I faked a little laugh from nervousness.

"Nothing. I noticed you have a dimple on your right cheek." He looked at me in a way I have never seen before. "You're beautiful."

"Oh, stop it, James." I immediately put my guard up and walked over to the edge of the bed and sat down. I was so used to my Dad, insulting my intelligence. It felt good to hear this type of compliment instead of the lustful, slimy comments I would usually get. My father didn't compliment me on my appearance. "You think so?"

"Yeah! You don't?" he looked at me like I was the dumbest person on earth. He sat next to me and paused for a moment like he was deep in thought. He turned and looked at me with that same look. I felt compelled to explain.

"Boys only want one thing from me. They take one look at me and forget I have a brain and feelings." I know it sounded like I was about to have a breakdown, but I was just exhausted. Trying to adjust to

womanhood without any shame seemed to be the hardest thing I have done so far.

"I'm not going to lie to you Marissa, I'm attracted to you, but it doesn't mean I don't realize there is more to you than just that." he got up from the bed and walked toward the window. *"And you need to realize that too, people only treat you the way you allow them to."* He moved the curtains; I suspect to see if Ms. James had gone back in.

No one has ever said anything like that to me before, not even my father. I stood up from the bed and took off my robe. I walked over to James by the window. I closed the curtains to get his attention, and he turned around and looked amazed and licked his lips. I walked toward him and took off his jacket, and it fell to the floor. He looked down at it falling, but I grabbed his face and pulled him in gradually and kissed him as softly as I could. I wanted him to feel his body fill up with the love I needed from him. He grabbed me and held tightly as our kiss deepened with each stroke of the tongue. Those kisses went deeper and deeper as he began to explore places he seemed to have already known. I felt myself filling with the desire I needed to have for him. We navigated toward my bed, and he laid on top of me, making sure he touched every part of me, and my passion grew to an elevation that I have never felt before. That's what I had for James, passion, and desire. He could be the one, but then maybe not.

It would have been nice to have been in love for my first time, but what did I know about love then? I knew I liked James a lot, but some of his qualities created some red flags that needed addressing. His arrogance was one, but I' wasn't afraid to check him if need be, so what the hell.
He lifted me and helped me out of my gown as I laid back on the bed, exposing my breasts. He started to caress and suck with extreme intensity. He sucked as if he was hoping some milk came out. I was so wet James went in me with ease to my surprise. There was some pressure but pleasingly. I wanted him, and the power of his thrust in me brought out another side of me. I moaned in satisfaction.

CHAPTER 4

The warmth of his love beside me each morning gives me the rejuvenation I need to carry on. Nathan has treated me with the respect that was, cliché as it sounds, sent from heaven. Each time I think of the move I decided to make with him to Houston, I rejoice. It was the best decision I have made in my life thus far. He is everything to me, and I will never forget the day he made me the happiest woman alive:

"I think we should just do it," Nathan said. After about a good nine months apart, once we moved here, it seemed he was just a bit hasty. Nathan came to see me out of the blue. He still had my number, and I had wished he had called, and that wish came true.

"Nathan, what are you talking about?" I asked.

"I love you; I want you to be my wife." He said it as if I should have known, and I did. Being with Nate made me want to be better;

for myself. He restored the love I thought I had lost. I felt delicate.

"Are you asking me or...?"

"I... I...," he took a deep breath. "I know I can't be without you." He said.

"Did you sleep with her?" I had to ask. I know how it is to try and move on from someone you thought was the one. Then, the whole thing blows up in your face because you knew deep down that it wasn't forever from the beginning.

He put his head down and took a deep breath. "I almost did." He looked back up at me with mercy in his eyes. "I realized I only wanted you, and I decided not to."

We just finished eating dinner on the rooftop of a popular restaurant in the city. He's romantic like that. I love the attention to detail from the flowering bulb lights to the laced napkins he chose. The soft kiss he gave after carefully seating me in the ambiance he created was perfect.

"Why so sudden, we've only been back in contact for what a week now?"
He grabbed my hand from across the white tablecloth that covered a perfectly round-shaped table for this moment. "Non-stop, might I add. I don't need an eternity to find out if I love you or not; I need an eternity showing you how much."

Dreaming and living is one thing but trying to believe in love is another. Either this was just a dream I was living in, or love has finally found me, and it is real. I began to cry.

We did not have a wedding or anything, and that didn't matter. We eloped that night and never looked back. As we made love that night, Nathan's bronzed, almond eyes glistened under the moonlight that was shining through the windows in our bedroom. He moaned with pleasure as we explored every inch of each other's bodies. His physique had deepened in color as it began to entwine with my complexion as we became one. Tasting him was like eating milk chocolate every night, and he became my addiction. He was my "peace," an excellent piece you would want to bite.

I still can't believe how your life can turn for the good when you began to love yourself. There was a time when I thought James was gold, and I was just the fool to chase after him. He shined in the daylight. I felt like he was the one for me, especially after giving myself to him. I was so naive. The ignorance of what is reality and what is not was in perspective with just one encounter with the past:

"Oh, hey Leah, longtime-no-see," I said. I heard about her friend, so I wanted to let her know I cared despite our differences. "Sorry to hear about Donnie, I understand you two were close?"

She had this frown on her face, and immediately her attitude showed its ugly face. This girl just could not have a pleasant thing to say to me since grade school. "Always a pleasure Marissa, always. Is there anything else I can help you'll with today?" I scoffed and shook my head a little. She could be a bitch sometimes.

James seemed like he was shocked, he could barely say anything.

"Oh, we fine," I added.

"Okay, that will be $5.47." she held out her hand to receive the money from James. I took a few steps over to look at a rack near the register. I picked up one of the VHS tapes to look at or pretended to be, but in the corner of my eye, I saw James and Leah. I could barely hear what they were saying, but it wasn't hard to figure out.

"Talk later!?"

I walked back over to where James was and grabbed the bag. I nudged him a little as an indicator that it was time to go, or there was going to be a problem. "Alright, girl, see ya around." With a sly smirk, I exited the store with James.

Once we got out in the parking lot, James started with his stupid questions because he knew I was mad. "Alright, Marissa, what's the matter?" He unlocked the car door, and we got in.

"You know damn well, James," I said as I put on my seat belt. I sat back with my arms crossed. "You were flirting right in front of me."

"No, no, I wasn't." he lied.

"Whatever, James, just take me home."

He paused a moment. "Fine." He started the car and headed home.

Those dark times allowed the light to shine in. Nathan is my muse, my inspiration. I love him with every bone in my body. He makes me feel like no other. I have learned to enjoy not only him but myself. He makes me laugh, he allows me to think and be free; free to be me. I could not ask God for anything more. I still have my anxieties and doubts, I am human, but nights like this all my fears are non-existing.

Nathan explored every inch of my body that night, he sucked and bit places I didn't know I had. He made sure nothing was left untouched. My body was an unconquered territory, and he was Matthew Henson discovering the North Pole for the first time.

"Arrgghh!"

We both moaned as we reached our destination, breathing heavily from the release of our love for one another. He held me tightly around my waist as I laid on him still straddled.

CHAPTER 5

"Babe, can you pass me a glass of that infused water?"

"Yeah sure," Nate said as he opened the refrigerator door to look for the batch I made yesterday. It was perfect for after our love session. He poured it in a glass and gave it to me.

"Thanks, Babe." I took a sip.

"Your welcome." He said with a little bow.

I thought it was cute. I know the one thing I did love, having a chef as a husband. Do not get me wrong; I can burn too, but, for some reason, the food tastes a little better when a man cooks it for you. Today, I am loving what Nate is serving.

"I got another hour before I have to be at the restaurant," informed Nathan.

"Okay, how long you think you're going to be today?" I know the weekends were late nights and early mornings, so it was hard to get the quality time we both needed.

"I'm not sure, you know I'm going in late so, you know how Kev is?" he sat down across from me on our island and started to eat his breakfast. He just had his pajama pants on and no shirt looking more scrumptious than this meal that was in front of me. "What?" he said while biting a piece of bacon.

"Nothing," I said, flirting a little. Nate must have caught me in a gaze. The way he looked at me aroused me, and I leaned closer over the island. We began to kiss passionately. I had the biggest smile on my face as I placed my forehead against his.

"Oh, nothing?" Nate got up from his side of the kitchen island and walked over to where I was sitting. He picked me up and sat me on the counter.

The intensity of his thrust, once he was inside me, was like I've never felt. Each time with him seems to be different than the last. I was almost at my peak of release when

Junior started to whine on the monitor. Nate was near his because I can hear it in his escalated breathing, and I know he was not going to stop. "Nate. The. Baby." I tried to slow him down.

"Yeah." he kept going. "One mo' minute, jus…a coup…mo…" Nate exploded. He tried to continue to stroke, but I was too far off by then, my mind was on tending to the baby.
"Jesus! Did you…?"

"No." I struggled to get from off the counter, breathing heavily. Nate looked exhausted. "I'll be back, clean that up." I trotted off laughing.

"Shut up." He said, laughing and breathing hard, leaning on the counter.

CHAPTER 6

It would not be a good morning if I didn't experience some heartache. I can remember my first time. My ignorance hit me like a ton of bricks to the head. How could I had been so dumb? But when you think you are experiencing a love like no other, you are bound to do anything you can to hold on to the feeling. James and I had just "made up" over the weekend after I confronted him about flirting with Leah. I felt like I was on cloud nine as I walked down the hall to meet him at his locker. To my dismay, after I turned the corner, I see James and Leah talking in the hallway.

I hid behind one of the pillar-like brick walls that were strategically placed to control traffic in the halls. Their body language, as they conversed, seemed more intense than it needed to be, and this brought on my fears of what I've been feeling all along:

"He gave me a ride. We do stay in the same neighborhood." I heard Leah say. "And honestly, I thought you would be too busy,

you know, with your new relationship and all.”

They started to walk away from her locker until James grabbed Leah's elbow, as to stop her, and said the most devastating thing, I could hear him speak.
“She's not my girlfriend if that's what you're talking about, Leah.” My heart skipped a beat, and I almost lost my breath. I could not believe what I had heard.

“Okay, it's your choice.” I heard Leah say. As I walked away with the most stunning look on my face, I was stopped in my tracks.

“Hey, Marissa, wait.” I heard James yell out to get my attention.

I kept walking as if I didn't hear anything to my class. At that time, I wasn't sure if I heard him call my name, or it was my imagination. All I wanted to do was remove my presence from this entire scene. That day was just the beginning of my “on-again, off-again” relationship with James.

"Are you almost ready?" I asked Nathan as he seemed to struggle to find anything of his.

"Yeah, I'm looking for my keys." He said, patting his sides and looking around. His adrenaline was so high. It was kind of sexy though to watch him go back and forth; the time he takes in the mirror putting on his uniform and adjusting his package. I tend to like that part a lot. "Have you seen them."

"I put them on the hook downstairs, where they belong," I said, wrapping my arms around his waist.

"Oh, yes, downstairs. I keep forgetting that." He kissed the back of my hand and went briskly down the small stairway to our living area to get his keys. I followed behind, slowly watching him zig zag his way downstairs as well. I picked up his jacket and handed it to him and stood while he put it on with my hands on both hips. He was giving me the eye acknowledging my presence before he must dart out of the door.

"See ya later." He gave me a quick but passionate kiss, then another. "Bye."

"Bye." I rubbed the side of his cheek as he backed up and turned to leave. He walked out of the door, and I began to pray as I always do when he would leave the house and hope he would make it back safely.

There have been many times in my life that I did not feel safe. Being raised by my Dad, I did have a fear of being harmed. This fear produced a perfectionist, and the embedded trait has followed me all through college.

I had stopped talking to James altogether. I was not about to be taken for a fool any longer. I enrolled in the nursing program and was getting along well up until about midway my freshman year. I would run every morning, hoping that by doing this, I would be able to avoid any negativity. I would run, pray, write something inspirational, and then get my day started. This one morning, I was on a nearby trail on my way back from a three-mile run. In the opposite direction, a guy was approaching; I could not make out the face, and he did not look like one of the regulars that I would see in the morning. I always carried mace with me, so I knew I'll have some type of defense. As he approached, his running slowed. I began to feel nervous and looked behind me, and there was no one in sight. I stopped running and stared his way. He began to walk toward me at a faster pace than before as if I was his target. I froze and couldn't think of my next move. Before I knew it, he was closer than he needed to be, I panicked and emptied the keychain of mace I had directly in his face:

"Ahhh!" he grabbed his face and fell to the ground. "What you do that for?" He struggled to get back up, and the closer I looked at this fool, I realized who it was.

"JAMES!"

Were my eyes deceiving me? At first, it was a feeling of relief that it was someone I knew and not some crazy man out to get me. Then, knowing who the "assailant" was, I wasn't so sorry. He got what he deserved. Maybe the mace would open his eyes, and he'll see what he lost.

"YEAH! Who did you think, damn Marissa, you had to spray so much?" he was rubbing his eyes uncontrollably. "I need to get somewhere to wash my eyes, like now."

"Okay, c'mon." I helped James back to where the dorms were to find a restroom to rinse his eyes. We finally got to an eye washing station that was in one of the dorms, and James vigorously washed his eyes. "Sorry." After I saw the damage, I felt a little remorse for spraying him unintentionally, but I had to confess to rejoicing in it a bit.

"It's alright." he wiped his face with the paper towels I found. "I figured you wouldn't recognize me with all this hair on my head."

James did look different, mature. It was attractive. "Again, I apologize for spraying you with my mace, I have to get ready for class." I began to walk away because I knew if I didn't, I would regret it for the rest of my life.

"Alright, no problem." James has a way of channeling your inner emotions and saying precisely what you need to hear to draw you in. "Hey, since I'm here now, maybe we can catch up?"

"I'm not sure if that's a good idea. I have so much going on now and..." I was not in the mood to deal with him right now.

"Look, I know, we fell off somehow. I'm not sure what I did but, is it possible to just clear the air between us? Go out with me, so we can talk? As friends?"

If I knew then what I knew now, I would have never had so much compassion and accepted his offer. Insanely, I did miss James. I missed those thoughtful phrases he would tell when we would have our phone conversations, that he seemed to never live by. I started back up with James after about nine months of him "running" into me.

CHAPTER 7

My favorite patient came into the clinic today, Ms. Washington. Her attitude was different, not the usual discouraging way she would appear. After getting her into the exam room, she began to tell me she was dating this sixty-five-year-old man that she met at the bus stop on the way to the pharmacy.

"Yeah, chile, I just asked him what he was doing sitting there all by himself, and we've been together ever since." A light smile appeared on her face.

I liked working around the elderly. If you just listen to the wise, a lot can be learned about life. What I've learned so far is that life is not about what is fair, it's about who is favored. All favor that we may receive is not equal, but we are still favored.

Even though I've been through hell and back, it seems, in such a short span of life, I still appreciate those trials and adversities that made me who I am today. I have everything I could dream of in life centered through love. Then, why do I still reflect on the past as if it will come to hunt me one day? Maybe I haven't forgiven myself of the things that have happened, or I have done in my past. I do believe in redemption, repentance, forgiveness, and from what Ms. Washington was telling me, I know for sure, regardless of what does happen in your life, love does come back around.

"Oh, wow, Ms. Washington." I smiled with a slight giggle. It was the cutest thing to me.

"Yeah, I know I'm 90." I imagined she figured what my amazement was about. We both chuckled. "Don't worry, you'll figure out who you are."

Her statement troubled my spirit a little, maybe due to my judgment of her relationship. I did not ask any questions, I mostly listen. "I sure hope so. I'll go get the doctor now." A 90-year-old with a 65-year-old? I thought. Its either one of three ways; he found a sugar momma, he is her caretaker, and she's maybe developing Alzheimer's, or they are genuinely in love.

Who am I to question the situation because the Lord knows what I have done for "love?":

"Come back to the room."

"No, why would I do that?" He must think I am a fool. "And for the record, please don't command me to do anything."

"Marissa, why must we do this every time, huh?" I could not believe how arrogant James was being. The fact that I just caught him with my roommate was the last straw. Before I went home for Thanksgiving break, I went over to James' room to finally tell him that it was over, and little did I know; the good Lord gave me a little help.

I was back in my room, awaiting the entrance of this crooked-headed whore. My phone rang to no surprise. "I'm not surprised to hear you say that, James." I was shaking my head at the nonsense on the other end of the line. "Just pretend nothing ever happens, just pretend you have no responsibility. I'm so sick of this, I swear."

He did a little chuckle. "Marissa, you've got to be kidding me. When did we determine that this was a THIS? Please let me know. You kill me sometimes. You act like you haven't been using me either."

That hit me like a brick somehow. I thought that I should be mad at the accusation and the derailment of the blame somehow. "What do my past mistakes have to do with what you're doing wrong to me in the present? You're such a manipulating womanizer, funny, just like Angie said about you a couple of weeks ago." I thought some more, trying to calm myself down as I paced the floor. I can feel the sweat on the receiver from the brisk run I just took and the adrenaline I wanted to keep to "beat the breaks" off Angie.

"Fuck You, Marissa."

Angie slowly opened the door to our room and stood with her back close to the wall. The door was cracked enough for a quick escape if she needed it. "How original. Goodbye, James!" I slammed the phone down and stood there looking at Angie, wondering should I smash her head in with it. "What can you, how can you, possibly? you're sad, so sad."

"Look, Marissa. First, I am so sorry. It happened so fast, but then I was going to tell you so that you can see." Angie said. She was standing with her hands up, ready to defend herself.
"So, you decided to sleep with the guy you know I'm in love with to show me that he's what I just called him. Who are you?"

Angie is still alive today; I couldn't hurt her because, in some twisted way, it did teach me to stand up for myself. I was too dependent on James and not on myself. I could not bear the thought of going back to him. That is why I was glad when it did come the time to close the chapter, I said exactly what I wanted to say:

"If things don't go your way, you throw a fit like somebody owes you something," James said, probably hoping to make me feel guilty for calling him out on his bullshit.

"Oh, oh, okay, James." I began to walk away and then turned back around. "You know what James, not one time you've considered how I feel in this whole situation, not even a sorry." I knew my responsibility in this as well, and I had already owned up to that. But he was to blame as well, and today, he will be taking responsibility for his actions. "You've used me, lied to me, and led me on. You were my first, and you had the one chance to do the right thing with love, but you made your choice to not take it. So, James, this merry-go-round you keep playing on with me has stopped because I have jumped off. I still love me more than you ever will. Now, Stay the fuck away from me. Good-bye!" A tear fell from my eye as I turned to walk away.

"Marissa, wait!"

I cringed at the sound of James calling me. His monkey ass needed to back off. My release of emotions healed me in that one moment, and I never looked back.

CHAPTER 8

Not just anyone can watch Junior as far as Nathan is concerned. I don't blame him for having that fear. I am sure every parent has that same thought. My mother-in-law watches our son on the days that Nathan is off from work. This way, Nathan can catch up on some sleep and still have time for the two of us. You can only take as much precaution as humanly possible, but you must let your children grow up.

Our son started going to the daycare after a whole year of trying to convince his father that it was okay. A three-year-old needs to be in a place with other children and a learning environment. I convinced Nate he would only go for a couple of hours. He agreed, but with stipulations:

"It's only for a year to see how he adjusts. Once he turns four, I'm taking him out, and my mother will be keeping him until he starts school. Problem solved."

"Is that your final...?" I couldn't get the last word in on this matter. I'm sure, later, I could persuade him otherwise.

"Final!" Nathan can be very stern in his decisions. When those decisions are based on the one thing he fears the most; failing as a father, he is especially careful.

After about a year, Junior was doing well at the daycare. Nathan was still adamant about homeschooling him. I encouraged Nathan to let him stay a little longer until he decides if he wants to permanently homeschool him or sends him to a public/private institution. Junior will continue to go if I have anything to do with it.

It was not a surprise for me to see them both up and playing around in the living room. Nate must have been well rested and could spare the energy. His mother was gone, which meant I was late. A patient fell in the clinic today, and I had to make sure the paperwork was done on the incident, and traffic was a mess on the expressway with its crazed drivers of the city.

"Well, hello." I stood at the edge of the family room, where toys were scattered. I danced around, dodging the foot traps as best as I could. The last thing I needed was to cut my foot. *"I am not cleaning that up."* I thought. But, most likely, I'll do it anyway. I developed an OCD habit of cleaning from the days I lived with my father. Now, I use it as therapy when I'm angry or stressed.

For a quick moment, Nathan turned around from playing with Junior. "Oh, Hey." He swung Junior up to pack him on his back and walked toward me. [kiss]

"How are you, you look like you're tired."

"Oh, thank you." I kissed my baby on the forehead while he was upside down somehow. "Hey, my big boy."

"You know what I mean. I didn't have to say you are the beat of my heart. You know this." Of course, he charmed his way out of it.

"Uh, huh," I smirked at his corny line a little. "Let me go take a shower and wash this "clinic" off me before I touch anybody or anything." I would always clean up first thing when entering my home. Working in a clinic, you can contract anything.

"Alright. I will get, well, we will get dinner ready. Isn't that right little man?" Our son laughed uncontrollably as Nate packed him to the kitchen. "C'mon, son."

He led him into the kitchen and started to take out pots and pans and seasonings. As I walked up the stairs slowly due to exhaustion, I thought about what Nate was going to come up with for tonight. "Alright, you two, be careful with him, babe, okay?"

"I got it, woman. Go upstairs and relax." He put Junior on the counter and started counting tomatoes with him.

I sighed deeply as I took each step toward our bedroom. My back and feet were throbbing from being on them all day. My clothes began to just peel off as I undressed while walking toward the bathroom. I could not get in the shower quickly enough. It was nice to finally have the feeling of home. I could relax, knowing that I finally have a loving husband and son, a family. I would have never thought I was going to have this type of life. Mom and Dad divorced when I was young, and my environment was not set up to where I was able to see the duties of a wife. Through my mother's actions, I vowed to never marry:

"Oh, hey mama," I was returning from visiting Leah in the hospital.

There was a man in the driveway leaning against a foreign car of some sort. I will never forget the look of my mother's face when she saw me pull up and caught her in the act. He got back in the car as she gave him a quick wave, and he took off down the street. "Oh, hey, baby, how you doin'?"

"I'm fine, how about you, momma?"

"Good, good." She started walking back up the driveway. She pretended to not know

what I was going to say next. I asked her, nevertheless.

"Uh, so who was that?"

She turned around toward me, and I felt a slight fear overcome me. "None of ya business, that's who that was, got it?" She said it with that same look your momma gives you when she knows you grown now, but not too grown to still get slapped.

"Okay, okay." Giggling a little, with my hands up, I surrendered to her soft but stern threat. I visit much more now since I was able to get a car from my Dad. He wasn't using it, and he figured I could. As a gesture of forgiveness for not being there over the years, is the reason why he honestly gave it to me. "Did you cook, momma, I'm starving?"

"Yeah, it's some greens and chicken wings leftover from last night." I opened the refrigerator, looking vigorously for the grub that was about to be devoured. "I think it's

some cornbread in there, as well." She looked back at me while going through her mail in the narrow hallway. The place looked much smaller than I remembered as a child. Coming back home put everything in perspective.

"Oh, it's cheat day!" My mother laughed as I continued to ramble through the fridge. She knew I could not resist eating something before I left. My weekly trips may be the reason why I can't get rid of this wheel barrel I drag around every day. Everyone has secrets they struggle with, and sometimes those secrets will bite you in the ass.

CHAPTER 9

Many women would love my life. A hard-working husband to come home to and a beautiful child should be a dream. I have a fantastic, fulfilling career where I get to make a difference in the lives of others. It sounds like happiness decided to come in my life and take over. Then why do I feel the need to be free? Maybe it's the effects of having the baby. My mother said it takes time to "feel like yourself again." With these hours between my husband and me, it's becoming routinely tiring.

I ran into an old friend at the grocery store today. During the time Nathan and I were on a break, I began to get settled into my new life with or without the possibility of Nathan not being in it. Do not misunderstand, I loved him during that time, but I was not going to dedicate my life to a maybe. I tried that before and lost myself for a moment. I did not want that to happen again.

"Oh. My. G- David?"

David was the one guy that I had wished I met before James. I probably would be on a different path in life or maybe not. Love tends to be a little better the second time around.

"Marissa?" he stood back and took a long look. A long look. I think because we were both stunned. "Wow! How have you been?"

"I'm okay." I paused for a minute. We both just stood in front of each other, swaying back and forth out of nervousness. Each of us trying desperately to reveal a believable smile of kindness. "You?"

"I'm good. It's been a while, huh?" David said, looking over toward my basket at Junior.

"Yeah." I laughed nervously. David was not pleased with my decision to choose Nathan. David and I met off campus at a nearby deli. He had a kind spirit to me, and his smile was sweet. It reminded me of my Dad on happier days; before the issues between him and my mom got worse. When he approached me in conversation, it was an immediate connection but not enough to break me away from my Nathan:

"Oh, I'm sorry. I need to be more careful." I accidentally walked into David while I was on my way out of the deli.

"No problem. You can bump into me anytime." He had a sly grin as he turned toward me as I was walking past. I just gave him a little smile and kept going out of the door. He was cute, but I was not in the mood for a conversation.

I made a right down the sidewalk and walked a few steps trying to unravel the Cuban sandwich I just bought out of the deli. I was starving.

"Excuse me, Miss?" I turned, and there he was with a slight jog coming toward me with what looked like my wallet. I could have sworn I put it inside of my purse before I left the counter. "Is this yours?" he asked, breathing a little heavy.

"Oh, yeah! Thank you so much." I took the wallet and looked at it, confused about how I could have misplaced it. I put it in my handbag along with the sandwich I purchased. I carry huge bags.

"No problem again."

"Well, it seems that way with you today, huh?" I pointed out.

He laughed and put his hands in his pockets. He had a captivating demeanor; it was easy to get lost in his light brown eyes. "It seems all my problems did disappear after seeing you." He held his hand out for me to shake it. "My name is David Wallace, and you are?"

I wiped my hand with the napkin I snag on the way out the door. "Marissa Orville," I said while shaking his hand. He had a firm grip but not that firm where it may raise a red flag.

David and I talked a little more and exchanged numbers. Over the next couple of months, we got to know each other as friends. He knew my situation, and at times he would try to convince me to forget about Nathan, but as I told him repeatedly, "David if you can't handle a friendship with me, then maybe we shouldn't be friends. You have to respect that."

He understood, and he did respect the boundaries we agreed upon, so things were going well. It was nice to have someone to hang out with while I was here in the city.

One day, Nathan decided to drop by my apartment. We had been communicating more, and it was looking like Nathan, and I wanted the same thing; each other. I hadn't seen Nathan in almost a year, but it seemed like an eternity. He walked thru the door, and I intuitively knew he was the one for me. The way he grabbed me, hugged me, and squeezed me; I could tell he felt the same. He was a breath of fresh air.

"I've missed you so much." We rocked from side to side in each other's arms. "How have you been?" he kissed my forehead.

"I'm better now." Nate and I had started communicating again and went out a couple of times before we decided to kill the bullshit and just get back together.

"Me too." I closed the door behind him and lead him over to the couch. We sat down and wrapped ourselves within each other and just held each other. It was nice to be in his arms again. For what was only a moment, seemed to be an eternity as I listened to Nates heartbeat while my head was on his chest.

[knock, knock, knock]

"Are you expecting somebody?" Nate asked.

"No." I sat up from the euphoric place that I was in and looked toward the door with a confused look on my face. *"I'm not sure who it could be at this hour."*

"Let me get it, just in case." Nathan stood up and walked over to the door and looked thru the peephole. *"It's a guy, kind of nerdy*

looking..." he chuckled a little as he looked back at me for my confirmation if I knew anybody with that description. I knew exactly who it was.

"Oh, that's David. I forgot we were supposed to hang out after class. You can open it." Nathan knew all about David. I didn't want to have any secrets between us.

"Oh, okay. I don't want to step on your toes. I'll step aside." He moved away from the door with his hands up, poking fun.

"Whatever, open the door, silly." Nathan opened the door, and David's eyes must have flown out of his sockets. "Hey, David, come on in." David walked in slowly with a distressed look on his face. "This is Nathan, Nathan, David." I walked over and closed the door. The guys were shaking hands and exchanging their hellos. "I'm so sorry, I forgot we were supposed to hang out. Nathan called, and you know..." I made a shy gesture as I looked at Nate. David did not look too amused.

"Oh, no problem. I just thought that, maybe..." He paused for a moment looking back and forth at Nate and me. I'm not sure what was going on in his head, but I can assure it was not good.
"Something happened to you."

"Oh, no. I am fine. I'm sorry again, I truly am. How about I catch up with you the day after tomorrow?" By now, Nate had walked back over to the couch and sat down.

"Uh, yeah, yeah. No problem." He responded.
I led him back to the door and said goodbye. David seemed confused as he left, but I didn't think anything of it.
"He didn't seem very happy," Nathan said.

"Why would you say that?"

"C'mon babe, he has a thing for you," Nathan responded.

"I mean we've discussed that already and he's aware of everything. I think since he's never met you, he was just making sure I

was okay. I mean, you haven't been around in the past eight months." I explained to Nate. I wasn't sure if I was trying to convince him or myself of the energy that David was giving off.

"Alright, if you say so. All I know, I'll be around more often to keep an eye on that one." Nathan assured me.

"Is that all you'll be watching?" I teased.

"Well, amongst other things." He leaned over and kissed me. My body temperature rose to capacity. We made love that night, and I had never felt more alive.

CHAPTER 10

"I hope you're not here to start any trouble, David?" I asked.

"Why would I do that?" He had the most impassive look on his face. I couldn't tell if he was upset, sad; he was hard to read. I began to get nervous.

"Well, we have to go, is that right Junior?" I pulled my son close to my chest and kissed him on the top of his head. As I stood in the aisle, full of fear but not letting it show, I looked David directly in the face. I wanted him to know that he would not intimidate me.

"You be safe out there, Marissa." He nodded and walked past me.

A cold breeze full of evil and hate whisked by me. I stood my ground and thought. *I've had fresher air in my day."*

I rushed home from the grocery store and locked all the doors and windows. I got Junior to settle in his room enough so that I can be alone to sort thru the many thoughts racing through my head. Juniors' unsettling demeanor was rattled by the type of energy that I was giving after running into David. As I paced back and forth, trying to decide whether to let Nathan know, I will never forget the day I found out that David was stalking us. Nate did warn me about my friendship with David, but I would have never thought he was the obsessive type. Of course, with my luck, I had to befriend him: *"Is this ole' boy in front?" Looking out the window of his apartment, Nathan tilted his head to the right in disbelief. We had just eloped, and I moved in with Nathan after graduating from nursing school.*

"In front of where and who are you talking about?"

"What's his face, um, Donald or...?" Nate tried to remember vaguely.

"David?!"

"Yeah, that's it." Nate turned toward me and pointed at his window. He slowly walked toward me with a slight grin. "This fool is outside on some stalking shit. How did he know where I lived?" Nate was upset, and it was all my fault that this was happening. "Are you fucking him?"

"Did you just ask me that, Nate?"

"All I'm saying, ain't no dude gonna be stalking nobody over nothing. I'm just sayin' Marissa." Nate made sense, but, in this case, it did not apply.

"I've NEVER slept with this guy, come on." I did an eye roll due to my annoyance of the matter. "I'll just call the police."

"Wait, let me see if I can reason with the idiot first."

"What?! Nate, please, I'm calling the police. He may be a full-blown maniac." I begged.

"Five minutes." I took a long sigh and swayed back and forth while Nate went and put on some shoes.

Reluctantly, I agreed. "Okay, five minutes!"

Nate went outside to see if he could find out what the issue was with David. I stood to watch by the window with my phone in my hand. Nate stood at the end of the sidewalk and made a gesture to David to come and talk. David got out of his car and walked over smoothly. He didn't seem threatening, but I was still in fear of his potential. Nathan began to talk as if he were trying to explain something to him, then abruptly, David stepped closer to Nate and was about three inches from his face. I immediately went to the door, opened it, and hiked down the walkway to the sidewalk with my phone in the air.

"Back off, or I'm calling the cops, David!" I yelled out. David looked my way with such anger and started to walk toward me at a fast pace. Nathan moved quickly in front of him and blocked his path to me.

"Hey, man." Nate put his hand toward David's chest to stop him.

"Don't touch me," David said to Nate as he pushed his hand away.

Nathan backed up a little and put his hands in prayer position. He was trying to hold his composure. "Look, man, as you can see, she doesn't want you here. After you cool off, maybe you can get an understanding of what I tried to tell you."

"Marissa." David pointed toward me as he backed up. "I'm outta here." He looked at me in disgust and chuckled a little. "Yall deserve each other." He turned and walked back to his car. Nathan stood outside, watching his every movement until he drove out of the complex. I stood there, still replaying the amount of rage David had in his eyes. I have never seen him like that before. It seemed he was contemplating killing me. My body was frozen, and Nate was standing right next to me, calling my

name. There was a touch on my arm as I turned my head toward the voice.

"Marissa, you alright?"

"Yeah, just a little shaken. I- I've never seen David like that before."

CHAPTER 11

"STOP! STOP IT! STOP!"

"Marissa! Babe. Wake up! You're dreaming!"

As my eyes focused on what was real, I was rocked back to life with Nate holding me trying to calm me down. Another dream of the horror of my past decided to show its evil head. I chose not to tell Nate about seeing David, but, since then, more dreams of my attack have visited me and were more vivid.

"I'm alright," I said, breathing heavily. "I'm okay."

"You sure?" he said while lifting my chin.

"Mmhm!" I shook my head, hoping that Nate would believe I was okay, but I was not.

I laid back down and took a deep breath. "I'll be back, you want some water or something?" Nate asked.

"No, I'm okay. I am." I took another long breath, trying to calm my nerves from the terrifying dream of my past. They seem to come to hunt me more often now than before.

"Alright." he opened the door and looked toward his right but then went left. His thought was probably to check on Junior first then go downstairs.

My head began to pound because of the reoccurring thoughts in my mind of my assault. I never told Nathan of it because I know he would try and find him, and only God knows what would happen.

"Hey, I brought you some water anyway." Nate was back in the room, sitting at the edge of the bed by my feet.

"Oh, thanks." I sat up in bed to receive my water. I gulped it, and it was refreshing and calmed me down a little more.

"You sure you're okay?" he asked, rubbing my legs to soothe me.

"Yeah, I'm alright. Stop worrying. It's just dreams that'll go away soon enough. I probably need to stay off the spicy food." I tried to explain without revealing the actual truth of my rape.

"Yeah, dreams." He wasn't buying it. "Why so sudden? I have never known you to dream like that. Almost three weeks ago, you were simply fine and now..."

"Fine?" I said, feeling inadequate. "I'm fine now, or do you not think so?"

"That's not what I meant. I am just worried about you. Where is all this coming from?"

"I don't know, Nathan. I'm tired so, let us just go to sleep and talk about this in the morning."

He took a deep sigh. "Alright, fine."

He got up from the edge of the bed and hit the switch for the lights. I can tell by the way he got into bed; he was still a little upset with me. Nathan could always tell when I was withholding something from him. I laid there trying to think positive thoughts so I can go back to sleep. I got out of bed and kneeled. I began to pray:

"Our father, the maker of everything good and perfect. The pain that I feel is too much to bear, show me your way," I took a deep breath. *"I want to be who you want me to be, who you need me to be! I'm not free from my trespasses, I'm still healing, and I need these memories to go away. Please set me free..."*

I continued to pray for some time. I finally got back into bed and fell asleep. I slept so peacefully, I got up the next morning early for some coffee. I felt like I could conquer this thing and never have to let Nathan know. Last night never happened.

"Good morning, dreamer."

Correction, it did.

CHAPTER 12

My thoughts began to reminisce about my childhood and my relationship with my father. As a kid, I would go with my mother for the summer, and my Dad would come and "visit" a few times during the two months I was there. He would only come by because he did not trust my mother at all. He was very controlling.
I asked him if it were okay if I just write him that way, I wouldn't have to see the arguments that he and my Mom would get into when he came by. My father was due for a visit during the summer, and I remember them arguing in the hallway, and my mother said something that triggered my father because he had balled up his fist and clenched his lip so tight, I thought he was going to bite it off.

He never did put a hand on her, but it seemed to take everything in him to not strike her. I think it was because I was standing there, or maybe he was so used to my mothers' rants, he pitied her:

"I'm gone, c'mon Marissa!" my father pulled my arm firmly as we walked back down the hall to the front door.

"Where do you think you're going with my child?" my mother grabbed my fathers' hand and pulled it away from my arm. She stood in front of my father and pulled me behind her. "Don't even try it. Go find you something to do, other than coming over here harassing me. You do this every summer, James."

"Jean, I ain't got time for this. Where is he?"

"Who?!" my Mom threw her hands up in the air. "Who, James, huh?"

I looked over and decided to sit down on the couch because it was going to be another long petty argument between my parents. The systematic way things would happen became second nature to me. My parents would argue for about thirty minutes. Once my Mom would finally calm him down, he would leave without incident. I would have to come to the door and say goodbye, and the cycle starts again.

"Good night, Daddy."

"Good night, baby. I Love you."

I didn't get much sleep the night before. I would doze off occasionally and then be quickly awaken by the most subtle sounds in the house. I got up and went downstairs to the kitchen to turn on a pot of coffee, feeling an eerie presence in the room. I walked over by the kitchen window to look out, and all I saw was the rustling of the trees and the sprinkler system watering the grass as it was timed.

As I stepped back from the window, a dark shadow passed by. Slowly I turned, my heart began to race, and I was startled.

"Ahhh!" I grabbed my chest and spilled a little of the coffee I had made for myself on the floor.

"What on earth, Nate, you scared me?!"

"I'm sorry." He was startled as well and held out his hands to try and help somehow. "I was just checking on you; couldn't sleep?" he looked around for a cup to pour himself some coffee.
"No." I thought I would just get up and get the day started. At least I can take my time before heading into work, instead of rushing. "I needed to get up anyway."

After I cleaned the spill, I made from Nate sneaking up on me, I sat down, and we finished our coffee together at the table.
"We haven't done this in a while," Nate observed.

"What, have coffee?" I laughed a little. I knew where he was going with the conversation. Nate wanted me to be home more or just stop working altogether. He wanted to start a family, and another kid was on his brain.

"Yeah, but together. It's nice, isn't it?"

I didn't disagree. It was nice to be able to sit and talk to my husband. I wish it were more often but not at the expense of me putting my career aside. Nathan wants children more than anything. He would have a house full of them if he could.

"You don't quit, do you?" throwing the conversation angle off a little.

Yeah, well..." Nathan leaned back in his chair with a look of concern on his face. Before he could really get deep with the thoughts that were brewing in his head, I could tell by the expression of lines in his forehead, I made sure to intercept them by any means necessary.

"Don't forget after your meeting today to pick up Nathan from school. You promised." I reminded him.

"Yeah, yeah, I know." he waved his hand a little. "Well, let me go ahead and get ready. If I go in a little early, I can be done in time to take Junior out somewhere before coming back home. You cool with that?" he put his cup in the sink.

"Yeah, that's fine." I'm always okay with it, but it is nice that he acknowledges my feelings as well. I can be a little overprotective of my son. My background with men has been a learning experience and a struggle. I just want to make sure Nathaniel Jr. becomes a respectable person, someone decent at least.

Nate gave me a big hug and kiss and headed upstairs to get ready.

I could not get the thought of seeing David the other day out of my head. It didn't seem like he was too upset, but I did not trust him.

The night when Nate confronted him was horrifying because I have never seen someone with so much hate in their eyes. I decided to call David to clear up any misunderstandings about that night. I was so nervous I was shaking when I dialed the number. The receiver almost slipped out my hand due to the moisture of sweat seeping through my pores:

"Hello?" his voice was sweet like I remembered on the day I met him.

"Hey David, it's me," I said nervously.

"Yeah, I know. What's up, Marissa?" he sighed as to edge me to get it over with. He was the type of person that was straight to the point, so that is why I was confused about the whole situation.

"Well, I was calling to see if you had time to talk about what happened the other night? I believe there are some explanations to be made." I wanted to let him know I did not approve of his behavior.

"Explanations?" he chuckled a little. "By whom?"

"David. Stop."

"No. You stop!" There was a pause between us as we realized our voices were

escalating. "Why did you call me, huh? What do you want?"

"Why were you so mad the other night?" I said out of desperation. It seemed David refused to explain himself. "How did you find out where we...he lived?"

"Marissa, if you don't know by now. You never will. Goodnight." He hung up the phone. The dial tone sounded like a trumpet sounding off as I realized I had lost a friend.

CHAPTER 13

My day ended with me picking up a double shift at work. One of the nurses didn't come in, so I decided to cover for her. She had kids as well, so I understood. It was late, so I went to check if I could have an escort to the parking garage, but security was on their rounds. Not knowing how long it would take to get an escort, I decided to head to the garage. It wasn't that far, and I did have my mace. A safety precaution that I started to practice back in college. There were too many females on campus getting attacked, and I was not interested in being another statistic.

I had finally made it onto the floor of the garage where I parked. As I headed toward that direction, I got an eerie feeling like a chill on the back of my neck; just like I had this morning. I turned slowly to see if anyone was there.

"Hello?!"

There was no answer, so I continued to my car with more of a brisk pace than before. I turned the corner toward the aisle where my vehicle was and heard something fall. It sounded like a pipe falling or maybe something passing in the pipes. The sound made me stop in my tracks, and I looked around to see if I could place where it was coming from.

"Jesus!" I held my chest and jumped. I stood there, breathing slowly before uttering. "I'm so sick of that cat."

I would see the same black cat wandering around the lot looking for scraps. Nobody had seen it when I mentioned it about a month ago, which made me a little crazy in the office. I jogged a little to my car this time. I got settled in and started the engine. I took a deep breath.

"Get it together, Marissa." I adjusted the rear-view mirror.

"DAVID!!!"

I couldn't understand what he had said, his voice was muffled because thank the God above my window was not down. He tapped on the passenger side window and scared me half to death. I was stunned stiff as a board, and I couldn't move anything. My heart was pounding, and I think I peed a little. Anyone would do the same in the position I was encountering.

I was still in shock. I knew I heard a mumble from David or something, but the fear that was flowing thru my veins cut off all my senses. "Marissa, you cool?" I finally grasped the question and shook my head slowly. "Can you roll down the window, please?" he gestured with his hands to roll down the window, and he looked a little annoyed. "I'm not here to hurt you. I just want to talk."

I contemplated just putting the key in the ignition and driving off, but what harm could he do from where he was, and I wanted to know how he knew where I worked. I was still breathing heavily. He put up his hands to show me that he didn't have anything on him. I still did not believe him, but it was a kind gesture of some type of assurance of making it out of this situation.

"What do you want, huh?" I had rolled the window down just enough to hear his voice.

"Marissa, I tried calling you, but you haven't... you know what? I need to tell you something." He hesitated.

"Tell me what?"

CHAPTER 14

I picked up Nathan Jr and took him over to my mother's. By the grace of God, I made it home in one piece. The way I was speeding on the freeway, it was nothing short of a miracle that I did. I got out of the car and went into the home that my husband and I created for ourselves. I stood in the doorway, and I could hear my husband run down the stairs, and to no surprise there, he stood in his work attire, wondering where our son was.

"Hey, I've been calling you. Where is Junior?" I walked down the hall and into the kitchen without giving him a second look. I was disgusted. "Uh, hello?"

I turned and faced him. "He's at my mothers'." I turned back to get a bottle of water from the refrigerator.

"Okay, and why is he there instead of here?" he started to become uneasy.
I turned around from the refrigerator. "So! How is Denise?"

"I beg your pardon?"

David had shared with me some disturbing news. I'm not sure how he knew what he knew, but I know it was not beneath me, nor was I naïve enough to not inquire about it. "Oh, you forgot who you're sleeping with? Wow!"

"Sleeping with? What? How?" he stumbled to say.

"HOW?! How what Nathan? How I found out?" I shouted as he stood there, speechless with fear and anticipation of what I may say or ask next.

"Marissa, I can explain…"

David's words were exact. I did not want to believe him, and I was hoping to prove him wrong. I was disappointed, and the reality fell like a ton of bricks from the sky:

"How do you know David? Is this just your sick way of trying to be with me?"

"No, Marissa. I would never do anything to hurt you. I saw them." He was so passionate in his response; it was hard not to think there was some truth to it. After all, before David started to develop feelings for me, we were friends, and I guess, even though he was disappointed in the way things had turned out, he still looked out for me. "I was sitting in the diner when I saw her walk in. I didn't think anything of it."

He went on to say that Nathan walked in, and he knew he recognized him. It had been a while since David and Nathan had words outside of his apartment, but he described Nathan from head to toe.

"Why didn't you just tell me when you saw me in the grocery store?" The way he was acting was weird that day, and maybe this information is what had him in a difficult place.

"I don't know, Marissa. At first, I wanted it to be bad karma for you, but then I couldn't let you go out like that. You had a son, a *family. The last thing I wanted to do was be the cause of a disruption in your life, in your son's life." His words were sincere in his confession, and at the time, I figured he did still have some animosity toward me. "When I saw him, I was going to leave because I didn't want him to remember me. But, when he went over and sat with the young lady, I decided to stay. I wasn't sure if you were still with him or not until I saw you in the store with your son. Which, by the way, looks just like him."*

My mind began to race. I started reliving all the moments from the day I found out he went to Denise for 'help,' and it all made sense. The long nights and days 'at work', the distant feeling between us. Nathan was more than just confiding; he was involved emotionally. I left David in the parking garage feeling lost under the assumption I was living a lie.

I walked over to the junk drawer in the kitchen and pulled out the past-due bill.

"What was this, an actual date, Oh, yall playing "doctor" now!?" I crumpled up the paper and chunked it at Nathan.

CHAPTER 15

My insecurities started to set in real deep after discovering this so-called "friendship" between my husband and this other woman. I wasn't cocky, but I for damn sure will not lose my husband to Denise Michaels. She was not a big girl, but she wasn't small, either. She had an attractive shape for her size. I had packed on some weight as well, and it has been hard getting it off, but on my worst day, I knew I could outshine this trash of a woman.

"I felt alone, and with you being gone working or doing the other million things you feel you, and I do mean you; alone, must do, it just happened, Marissa." Nathan had backed me into a corner. "I felt you didn't care!"

What, I didn't care? The way I get up at the crack of dawn every day just the same as he does, and he dares to say that '*I didn't care*'? Why was he *really* reaching out to Denise instead of me?

"Humph!" I scoffed at his lame way of trying to turn the tables.

He followed me into the living room. He was following me like a lost puppy dog that you fed once and now won't leave. Nathan was thinking of every excuse and explanation he could come up with to rid my mind of his exposed secret.

As I sat in my living room across from him, I can sense the dismay that has engulfed our marriage in just one day. I couldn't do anything but ask him about the day he decided to be with me instead of her. All I wanted to know was this a lie from the beginning. Has he been continuing to be in contact with her? Or, has it been that rough of a road between us?

"No, I have not been in contact with her since. I love you, not her."

To hear him say the words 'I love you' made me cringe. I have never heard it that way before. The phrase 'I love you' should make you feel warm, cared for, and assured that this feeling, let alone a person, will always be there for you to lean on or to reach out to for help. I began to cry.

"I can't BELIEVE you would do this to me?" yelling out my frustration in the palm of my hands.

I rocked back and forth on the couch with my arms folded, and tears started to form even more. My mind started racing back to the times we shared. The more I tried to remember everything we have been thru and trying to see where we went wrong, the more heartbroken I got. I could not look at him.

"It was just." He paused and tried to come a little closer. He sat down next to me and tried to grab my hand, but I refused. I refused to be coached into thinking it was alright. I guess even in marriage finding true love is a battle within itself. "Our lives moved so fast. I felt like I didn't have a handle on things." With his head held down, I can see the humiliation of his actions has made him quite humbling.

"A handle on what, Nathan?" I looked at him and braced myself for this crock of shit.

"Marissa, we got back together, got married, working all times of the day and night, the baby, uh, uh, uh; opened the restaurant…" I thought he was going to go on for hours. It has been a lot on us with our lives changing so suddenly. But he knew this or did he not. We are both young adults trying to "grow up" and become who we are supposed to be in this life. Just like I became his wife, I cannot be his wife. "All this in a matter of five years. I was stressed, and I couldn't talk to you."

"Here we go with that 'You can't talk to 'me' mess.' When did you try, huh, because I don't remember that?"

He scoffed a little and stared straight ahead. I continued to wipe the tears that have now fallen down my face. "I'm working, you're working…"

"Yes, I am! You're not in this by yourself, and what you're in, which is a marriage, is with me." He really thinks that having a family to look after and then, being the head of that family, is an excuse to have for possibly breaking up a family. I began to get a headache. "I can't deal with you right now. I need you to get out." I wanted to beat the hell out of him.

"Are you serious?" Nathan stood at about six feet tall. His sudden reaction standing up from the couch made me heed the potential that this may not go down the way I want it to. I stood up as well.

"Yes. I cannot think with you around or near me right now. Please leave." Stepping back, I pointed toward the front door of our home. "Just. Leave."

I would not know what a loving home is, even if it had fallen on top of me, like the wicked witch of the east. I remember the day the abstraction of a home, that I created in my mind, was ripped from me like the shirt that was torn from my mother the day she decided to leave:

"You think you can leave me?" My mother and father began to tussle. I was standing in the doorway, screaming to the top of my lungs. The sonar of fear that I was spewing out did not make my parents cease from the disgraceful example that can ever happen between a man and a woman.

It seemed like I was in a dream the moment I saw my father backhand my mother across the face. She fell back, and the sound of her shirt ripping seemed to pierce me directly in the heart. "Fuck You, James!! You ain't neva have to worry about me again! C'mon baby!"

My mother got up off the floor. She touched the side of her face and looked toward me, crying hysterically. "Stop, Mommy Stop!" She grabbed my arm to pick me up, but my Dad overpowered her and took me out of her arms.
"You not taking her, she doesn't need to be with you." My father stood in front of me as

if he were protecting me from another life form. "You don't even know who you are today."

"How dare you?" My mom walked toward my Dad as if she were ready to throw another punch, but something seemed to take her breath away. She just tightened her lips, turned, and walked toward the door. "I'll be back, baby, I promise. I'll be back for you." She blew me a kiss and walked out the door.

I wasn't sure what my father meant at the time, but as time went on, I figured it out. My mother suffered from mental illness. She would sometimes go into these episodes of depression, and then the next minute, be the happiest person alive. She would never harm me. The most I've seen my mom do is fuss at my Dad on how she could not stand his controlling ways. Regardless, it was the unhappiest day of my life.

CHAPTER 16

It had been a week since I've heard from Nathan after asking him to leave. I will admit, it has been agony not being able to sleep next to him at night. My days were starting to run into each other from the lack of sleep. I did not see the need to call Nathan after what he had done, but I would have thought he would have tried to call and check on his son, to say the least. Secretly, I still had that desire to be loved by him, and I knew that my son would open the door for communication if he had not come by sooner. After, what seemed to be an eternity, there was a knock on the door.

I didn't know too much about her, even though we did all go to the same school. However, Denise was in forbidden territory. She was a real southern bell with a slick city personality that was dying to get out. She ran down the halls often, back and forth to this club or this activity, the overachieving type. Was I jealous of her? I admit it, at times, I was. Maybe she was the type of woman that Nathan needed, or perhaps he had grown tired of me.

She seemed to have figured this love thing out, but from what Nathan told me, she was quite selfish in her approach. She wasn't willing to try. They were young; we all were but someone like her, I do not believe she took him seriously.

I lit a cigarette from an old pack I had in the kitchen drawer. The anxiety I felt was unimaginable; I became numb as the doorbell rang.

My heart jumped for joy but then skipped a beat from the fear of what was waiting on the other side of the tall framed door. Was this going to be the entrance or exit of the life I loved? Loving Nathan did not seem like an option until now, and I was not enjoying the choice of having that privilege. I walked out of the kitchen and slowly down to the foyer. I took a deep breath as I peeped out of the side window, and there he stood. Hands in his pockets and head held down, he took a deep breath as if he had been practicing for a big performance. I slowly placed the curtain back in its original position and touched the door handle. It was cold. As that same coldness of air washed my face when I opened the door, the image of my husband stood before me in a different form. He was different, and by the look on his face, I was different. Reality hit like a ton of bricks as we looked at each other eye to eye.

He stood there in his tall stature, obviously nervous. I could tell by the way he could not make eye contact long enough to let me see deep into his soul. I could always know his thoughts just by looking into his eyes.

"Hey."

Nathan's expression was of sorrow from the top of his kinky fresh styled hair. He smelled like the lightly scented oils he often used, for which the wind blew directly in my face. I was tempted to jump on him and devour him as if I haven't had chocolate since last Spring. I placed my "big girl" face on; no-nonsense, from the top of my curly 'fro to the tip of my nose, which glistened under the sunlight, I'm sure. I made sure I was always ready. Nathan is my life, and I knew this day would come, eventually. Leaning against the heavy door of our home, my frame sent rays of lust, or so I thought, toward his way. I wanted him.

"Hey."

"I want to come back home."

How dare he have the audacity. No compassionate speech, no pleading with me, or some indication that he cared about MY feelings for once. Nathan could be overbearing in his approach, only thinking of what he wanted all the time. It was always all about him, not today. I was fed up.

"Well, it seems you have a problem." Thinking of the image of him and Denise bouncing up and down in a godforsaken motel made me want to throw up. "This is not your home anymore." I folded my arms in pure judgment. He was not going to charm his way out of this one.

"You can't be serious." I was astonished by how he thought otherwise. "So, we can't try to work this out somehow?" his question penetrated me as his eyes looked upon me intensely as if he wanted to reach inside of me and take what he was so desperate for. He wanted my heart to use and my mind to control.

"I'm not sure what to be serious about Nathan. I may have my faults, and I cannot blame you for your sins any more than you can blame me for mine. As a wife, I tried my hardest to do what I thought was right. Yes, I worked a lot of hours, but our child was clean and fed and was well taken care of."

Balancing everything did become overwhelming. I began to wonder if not staying home, as Nate wanted, led to me neglecting my husband.

"But I will not be manipulated into thinking everything is okay, and I shouldn't want better."

"I still love you." His word struck my heart like a musician plucking his guitar. I believed he did love me, but where do you draw the line between love and being a fool. Should I neglect myself for the sake of love?

CHAPTER 17

When you love someone, you tend to do things that you usually would not. How can love, something that is supposed to show patience and kindness, can also bring out frustration and animosity? It's all too confusing, but I'm drawn to it. Love is my addiction.

I could not imagine being alone. I want someone to hold me and tell me it will be alright. I wanted the peace that I never felt as a child; that I so long for as an adult. Nathan provided that feeling and this feeling, I named love because that is what I needed.

"I promise I will never hurt you again." He would say.

I thought a husband was supposed to teach me, care for me, fight for me, protect me. Even though time had created a distance between us, I still needed his presence. I tried to believe his words. I wanted to absorb them into my heart, so they can pump thru my veins to keep me alive, but I couldn't. My faith in Nathan changing his ways was not substantial, but I allowed him back into my life. We had a child together, which was the excuse for my toxic decision. My resistance to believe and respect my husband as my husband began to fade, and as quickly as it disappeared, the revelation of who Nathan indeed was, became crystal clear.

It was evident that Nathan was unhappy even though he practically begged to come back to his family. Something else had possessed his inner being, and he slowly deteriorated into a man that I did not recognize.

I could not move, I couldn't breathe, I didn't know what to do. I struggled to free myself from the grip Nathan had around my throat. I managed to kick him in the groin area to free myself.

"Aarrgh!" he stumbled back, holding his "package." A "package" I enjoyed receiving on-demand every time he asked.

As he stumbled back, he gripped my necklace of the crucifix I bought for myself while in college. I can feel my heart being taken away from me in that same instance. I could barely see the chain but the scratch that was on the back of my neck, from him ripping it, and the way he regained his balance and looked down at it, made it seemed he knew he had gone too far. I would pray daily; it appeared, for some type of resolution in my marriage. I wanted my God to guide me thru this adverse time, but it seemed I was not in favor. Honestly, I did bring this upon myself.

I remember the day I bought my necklace. I felt so proud that day. I felt so golden that I seemed to glow. As the chain was placed around my neck so gently, I felt a sense of upliftment. I felt my burdens being lifted and brushed away as a cool breeze does when it is passing by, traveling to another poor soul who may need a fresh start. A breath of fresh air. Fresh wind.
"Is that the one?"

"Yes. This is it." After going thru what it appeared to be a hundred necklaces, I can sense in the tone of his voice he was getting impatient.

David and I had been hanging out a lot, purely platonic. I enjoyed being around David. He was a positive soul and seemed to "get" me. We could talk about nothing for hours and still have plenty more to share with each other. He was a true friend. I must admit, I wasn't sure if Nathan and I connected like David and me, but I was willing to make sure that happened. I was still in love with Nathan, and David was aware of this.

"I think she's finally made her decision." It was my birthday, and I wanted to treat myself for once. All I did was go to class and then to my part-time cashier job at the school bookstore. I made sure I stayed focus on my studies, or maybe I used it as an excuse to distance myself from myself. If I stayed busy, I didn't have to deal with my personal issues.

David placed the necklace around my neck, and I felt pretty, valuable, noticed. "Oh, wow," I whispered to myself. I can hear another customer ask the price of a ring that was a few steps over at the next counter. I looked her way, and she glanced and smiled. She mouthed to me 'nice' in an approving way. I looked back into the mirror and saw David smiling back at me as he always does. His smile was, I must admit, like no other. I glowed from the inside out.

When I know I am about to hang out with him, I do get a little excited. He is my friend. I didn't want to mess up anything with Nathan while on this hiatus, and I wanted to prove I can stay true to whom I say I love. I believe David is supposed to be my temptation, and I was determined to pass this test for a chance to be with Nathan.

"I got it."

"What?" I leaned back a little while looking into David's eye thru the mirror. He touched the necklace on the back of my neck, and I can feel his fingertips. It made my back

flinch, my muscles so happen to tighten, but there was no pain from the strain of this spasm.

"The necklace Marissa."

I began to see David in a different light. It was not because he offered to buy the necklace for me; it was the way he would say things. The look he gives when translating the most loving thing I've heard out of a man's mouth. I could not get caught up.

"Oh, that's okay, David. But thank you." I walked away from the mirror and back over to the counter area, where I first saw the necklace. My avoidance of his nice gesture was unmistakable.

David continued to stand in front of the mirror, looking toward my direction. His face showed disappointment.

"I'll take this one." I unhooked the necklace and gave it to the store clerk who was watching my every move. I didn't care; I was

more concerned about David, who had just walked out of the store. I could tell the disappointment in his body language. With his hands in his pockets and head down, he looked like a sad kid. He kicked his right leg a little, maybe kicking a rock.

"Alright, you're all set."

I paid the clerk, and she handed me my necklace. I was still in a joyous mood even though I knew I just let my friend down.

Nathan threw my necklace on the dresser and walked out of the room. His cockiness and need for control were on display. He acted as if he did not just have his hands around my neck, trying to choke the life out of me. I slid slowly off the bed, crying my eyes out and breathing so hard I can see my chest going in and out vigorously. This was the moment that made me realize I had to get out.

My Dad was controlling, but he only laid a hand on my mother one time. She was in a whirlwind of one of her "episodes." They would argue to the point where it seemed as it was going to get physical, but my father never has gotten to the point where he felt the need to hurt my mother. He was more of a mental abuser than a physical one.

I heard the door slam as he left. I did not care where he went if he was far away from me. I sat on the floor with my head buried in my hands. I felt a light touch on my forearm, gentle. The warmth of his body as he sat next to me, seemed to comfort me and brought me back to reality. I wrapped my arm around him and put Nate Jr in my lap. He turned and wrapped his arms, full of love, around my neck. The same neck that was under pressure a moment ago fighting off the hate and control that Nathan wanted.

CHAPTER 18

I flew back on an airplane back to Louisiana. Not sure why I decided to go back home. I could have easily stayed in Texas and found a place where I could raise Nathan Jr. Nursing brought in good money, but I needed a safe home, at least for the moment. There was an excellent offer in D.C., but I didn't know anything about living that far north. I took the safe route and stayed where I was familiar. Comfort was my only medicine.

We passed by the corner store that I used to run back and forth to for Dad. When he and Momma separated, he seemed to not fathom the thought of him doing what he called "women's work." These old traditions used to pester me each waking moment living with him. I always wanted to be noticed; to feel important. I was on the way to see my father, whom I haven't seen in years. Passing my old elementary school, where I thought I was the queen of all, made me recall why I mistreated Leah when I first met her, the good early days.

I saw people walking on the sidewalks going where the day planned for them to go. We began passing a carwash that took the place of the old laundromat nearby. I could see this beautiful woman who reminded me of my mother when I was younger. She was of a dark complexion, and she glistened in the sunlight. Her hair had been pressed but not so sleek to not show her real roots; bouncy. She stood with her hands on her hips, giving the man with a piece of paper in his hand an attitude it seemed.

I looked out the window at the trees that passed in the reflection of the sunlight. I caught another whiff of the cab's scent, which brought me out of my nostalgic state. It smelled of old leather mixed with every person in the country. I rolled down the window. It was late February, and the down south winds blew in the car window, clearing out any odor that may have been left behind from previous riders.

Cabs were not a big thing growing up, so I've only needed to call one a few times. My

Dad always provided transportation during my childhood. Our neighborhood was a decent black neighborhood with the occasional white family. I never knew how it was to really depend on public transportation until I was finishing up nursing school.

We pulled up to the home I first knew. The outside had been painted a different color, much brighter than I remembered. The creamed-yellow house made me feel that everything that was on the inside of it had to feel the same way it looked; welcoming and gentle, unjudged. The yard was groomed with hedges that seemed to be done by a professional barber rather than a yardman.

The house seemed put together, not one thing out of place. But I knew the truth of the inner walls. I often would drift back to those memories and needed an outlet, someone to talk to. Therefore, I befriended David after leaving Nathan, and he was there during the hard times of adjusting to life without Nathan.

"Okay, we're here, that'll be $109.32." The cab driver had his hand out as he impatiently waited for his payment.

David reached into his pocket for his wallet. He was dressed in a grey suit with a black trench coat. It can still be chilly this time of the year with the high winds off the gulf coast nearby. Winters were not endured long down south. The sunshine was our typical weather, and at these trying times, during these winter months, the wind can bring up old dog bones. The truth is I was not sure if the outside of the house that looked so bright, held the grave.

"Thanks." David's scent grazed my nose as his arm returned so he can put his wallet back in his back pocket. It was refreshing.

I felt in the end, whichever path I take in life, it will be alright. There was someone there, a helping hand. David and I got off to a rocky start in our friendship, but it turned out what I needed in my life was available all along, all I had to do was just grab it and embrace it.

The house began to not look so intimidating. This is the place I called my home for part of my life. The front door opened, a salt and pepper bearded man with a light covering of the same all over his head stepped out of the house. I needed to start over from the beginning, and in my eyes, he was the only original blueprint I knew, my Dad. His face was more humbling than usual. It yearned for assurance.

I stepped out of the car to the visual and was taken back a little. I had not seen my father in so long, I wasn't sure who I might really meet. How has he changed? Has he changed? Will he treat me like the little girl that was taken away from him long ago? Will I be afraid? Or will I fight back on what I believe and stand on? I am a grown woman. Should I care what he thinks?

I haven't heard from him but once since the last time I laid eyes on him. Momma started saying things to me back then that did not make sense. I was afraid, and my thoughts began to race:

"Don't ever come back!" Shoes, belts, and other articles of my clothing were being thrown at me. It was another episode of Momma feeling caged. She would get these episodes where she wanted freedom. From what, I don't know. But she would take it out on me, and this day I could not take it anymore.

"Well, let's see what he says." Walking down the stairs, I was filled at the brim of disgust. At my age, I should have been thinking about a college, prom, but instead, I was dealing with a bipolar mother and a father who was so passive-aggressive, he seemed to be a brick wall.

My Mom just told me that my Dad is not really my Dad, but my stepdad. She didn't know who my father was. While in the military, Mom had a one-night stand with another soldier, was the story. She was a virgin and was not taught anything about sex. It just didn't come up. She was sent off by her parents, just a naive little girl, no common knowledge of the outer world. Her parents were strict, and she was only taught the world from their view.

She ended up pregnant and decided to keep me instead of getting an abortion. She met my Dad while pregnant, and he stepped up. That's the kind of guy my father was, but the other part of her story was tainted. I didn't believe her.

"Hey." His rustic voice yelled out from the porch, and I was filled with anxiety. I wanted to turn back around and get back into the cab, but David took my arm along with Nathan Jr to encourage me on.

"It'll be okay." It had been over a year since I divorced Nathan Sr, and I needed to relocate. He began to stalk me because of his anger for me, ending the marriage. I remember one time waking up to my car being gone along with his nonstop calls using Nathan Jr as an excuse to continually come by or meet me somewhere.

"C'mon little man, don't be afraid," David said to Junior. We began to walk down the cemented walkway toward the front of the house. It had shrubs planted in every other square, as stated before, nothing out of place. Being in the military made my Dad very systematic. *"Everything has its place,"* he would say.

Perfection was what my father seemed to seek. I must say, I did pay particularly close attention to the way I dressed today and ensured everyone looked presentable. I remember getting critiqued by my father every day. *"sit up straight, don't eat like that, fix your clothes."* I believe he meant well; he just didn't know how to be soft. In his day, men were not to show emotion, it was a sign of weakness.
"My angel!" he said with his arms stretched out as he walked down the few steps to the porch.

I used to sit on the house steps many days, combing thru my thoughts as I detangled my hair. He had the biggest smile on his face as if we had been old friends.

"Dad. Hey." I felt awkward hugging my father.

I wasn't sure if I had moved on from my childhood. I have learned that the road to forgiveness comes in different forms. The paths we take are sometimes our own, and then love decides to reroute your life in a different direction. It was refreshing to see this new person that my Dad had become but bittersweet. My father was knee-deep in debt and needed us to stay with him to pay half the mortgage. In my mind, I did wonder was that the only reason he was so kind. That is not a positive way to think about a parent but, hey, they are people too. He is my Dad, but he is also James Orville.

CHAPTER 19

I was on my own now and needed a place to live for a month or two while I started my new job and began a new life. It was scary at first. Things had changed so much, and I hardly recognized the place. I wondered if I really fit in around here anymore. The house was pretty much the same. There was a new coat of paint or two throughout. The same furniture still existed and look rather good, considering it was the same furniture my Mom and Dad had before I was born. My father was a true believer. *"If it's not broken, then don't break it."* He would say. I would always battle with him on his one-liner words of wisdom. One time I responded by saying, *"Do you mean 'then don't fix it?"*

"See, that's how much you know. You don't have to tell me to not fix something that's not broken, but you do have to tell me not to break it in the first place."

Oh, to challenge my father, I had better have all my ducks in a row. I am sure he knew the significance of the saying, but he always looked at things with a different lens.

"There's my grandson." He stood back to take a long look at Nathan Jr, hands on the back part of his hip, his head cocked to the side. We stood in the foyer area of the house, where I would keep my pet hamster when I was younger. My Dad did not want it running all over the house, so he made a designated spot for his wheel by the front door. "He has your eyes, Marissa." I returned from my trance into memory lane long enough to answer.

"Oh yeah, I get that a lot." I continued to look around.

I'm not sure what I was looking for. Maybe a feeling, a sign that I was doing the right thing. I began to overthink as I always do. David and Dad were chit-chatting at the front area of the foyer. I walked a little ahead toward the stairs, looking around, absorbing the place I knew too well.

There was a wall full of pictures of Mom and me some years ago. I stood and stared at the pictures. The frames were all spaced out beautifully. An entire wall full of art.

"No, no, Junior, come back down." I lifted Junior off the stairs back on to the floor. He was getting restless from the ride over, and it was time for a nap.

"Oh yeah, she'll be fine. Come by anytime." My Dad told David as they walked toward where I was standing. I could not make out what they were saying previously. I was too busy in my own thoughts of the yesteryears, I presume.

David approached me and guided me aside privately. "Hey, I'm gonna go ahead and get out of here, the meter's running. You know where I'll be, so call me if you need anything. My plane doesn't leave out until the day after tomorrow."

"Yeah. Yes, I understand. You go on ahead."

I'm not sure how I would have made it without David's help. He had a strange way of letting me know what was going on right under my nose, but I was still grateful. His feelings of rejection and his love for me was a battle each day, he tried to explain to me:

"I hated you. I felt you used me, but then, I couldn't be mad at you. I knew up front what the deal was. Marissa, I loved you the first time I laid eyes on you and didn't know what hit me."

Nathan and I had been separated for some time, now going back and forth with legal matters. I decided to call David, and we met at a nearby café. It wasn't that crowded, very quaint. It was the perfect spot for a needed conversation in my life.

"I guess in a way, I can see your resentment against me, David. You were a comfort for me then. I just thought if I were honest about everything, upfront, it would be okay; we would be friends, and nobody's feelings would get hurt."

My view of things back then was cynical. I was too busy trying to survive and not go down the wrong path. I forgot to take David's feelings into full consideration for which was not a good quality in a "so-called friend."

Through it all, he was still here for me and was always my friend. He helped me sell the house and move back home. I told him about how my Dad was growing up, and it made him a little uneasy. Everyone has a story, and I didn't mean to reflect on my childhood as being this dark and depressing time. I tried to reassure him there was no need for him to be alarmed, but he insisted on flying down with us.

"Alright." he looked at me once over, and we hugged each other for a while. It was not a goodbye, but more of a see you later. Nate Jr grabbed David's hand. Every time David rubs the top of his head in that loving way, he does. "See ya, champ."

"Go on. Get outta here. We'll be fine." Urging David toward the front door with my hip, my Dad yelled out from the kitchen, waving.

"You take care."

David returned a high wave back to my father with a nod of understanding. I was right behind him, feeling a bit nervous about his departure, knowing that once he leaves, I will have to deal with the reality of my situation. The fact that I felt alone, frightened of what life is going to bring me and I wasn't sure if and will I be ready. I needed David once again for comfort, for shelter.
He headed toward the door, and I began to sigh deeply. The essence of his cologne that was gently sprayed over his chest this morning was in the air.

"Let me get the door. It can be a little tricky." We both smirked nervously. We both wanted this whole scene to be over, but then we both wanted to hold on a little longer. We comforted each other one last time before he headed down the porch steps.

"That's a nice boy." My father was standing in between the kitchen entrance and the foyer leaning on the wall slicing an apple. I would always be afraid when my Dad would pick up a knife when I was little. I was terrified then, but not so much now.

"Yeah." The breath I took help release some of the pressure of what was ahead, "Wha' cha' got to eat daddy," and a hot meal wouldn't hurt.

CHAPTER 20

"Are you my father?"

I stood on the steps of the porch looking upon the face of the man that I called father for the past thirteen years. A man I thought had the same blood running thru his veins as me. If he is not my father, will this explain his rigorous nature toward me growing up? If I wasn't his kid, why the need to stay and help raise me?

"Yes. That's all you need to know." His answer was cold as usual but with conviction. I felt he was hiding something from me. My stare must have plucked a nerve. He put his hands on his hip and looked up passed where I was standing. He began to turn away and paused for a moment. "Go on to your mother." He walked toward the front door of the house slowly.

If I did know the actual truth, would my life change somehow? All these thoughts occurred, and I didn't know who or what to believe.

"Are you crazy?" I heard my Mom in the background.

I turned and saw she was standing by the car, looking afraid and frustrated. She must have followed me after I stormed out of the house. We didn't live that far from our old home, only about a mile or two. "Get in the car now, Marissa!"
I had my Dad in plain view watching every possible sign of body language as he opened the screen door to the house. I wanted to see a sign that he was lying to me. I wanted to see a sign that he was telling the truth as well. I was confused. Usually, I could sense my father's emotions thru the resilient way he communicated.

I turned and walked toward the car, not glancing an inch toward my mother. She got in the car, and I can feel her glaring at me as she started the engine. I continued to look straight ahead; my face frowned up. I wanted my mother to see I was not in the mood for a lecture of any kind. She put the car in drive and drove from the curb abruptly. I wasn't sure what was to become of this day. I wasn't sure if I had found out the truth, but, at the end of the day, what I do know is, he was the only father that I knew.

The dinner table was silent for most of the meal. This was a reminder that some things do not change. My Dad was not much of a talker, but what he did say was profound. I had so many questions going thru my head; I became dizzy.

"I'm done. I can get the dishes."

"Hm." He looked up from his plate, where he was cutting into his steak. He looked as if he was surprised, I was here. I guess living alone, you can tune out anything outside yourself.

"I'm going to bed; I have a lot to do tomorrow." I got up from the table and pushed my chair in. Nathan Jr was picking at his plate and mainly playing with his GI Joe toy.

My father sat there in his usual chair and did not utter a word. I still had questions on whether he was my biological father or not, but I was dealing with too much already and didn't want to add any more stress to my life as it is.

"Let's go, son, so I can get you cleaned up. Say 'night-night' to Paw-Paw."

"Sleep good, little man. I'll see you tomorrow." My father's humble manner surprised me. I remember getting one-word sentiments. Maybe he had changed over the years. Getting older comes with change, so why not.

I walked Junior to the room where we would be staying for the next few months. It was the old guest room where all our relatives would stay when they were in town. It was still made up the way my Mom left it many moons ago. The beige wall color was a little darker now, or maybe it was the lack of light in the house. The first thing I did before preparing dinner was open all the windows to bring some life into the place.

My surroundings were not bad on the surface, but I believe these walls held a far more unsettling reality. Loneliness. My father had lived alone, from the day I questioned him about being my real father. That day was the last time I saw him in the presence of a woman. I never saw him with another woman or even a friendly flirt within the passing of a woman. He and my Mom had their trials, but I believe it was not so bad to where he would just give up on love.

"C'mon buddy, let's get you dressed."

I walked junior out of the bathroom after drying him off. He put on his pajamas and grabbed his favorite stuffed animal. It was a little monkey with the nerdiest glasses. I thought it was adorable, so I picked it up for him at the drug store a year ago. He hasn't let it go since.

I got Nate into bed comfortably. His eyes began to drift into another land as I read the words from his favorite book for the third time. I made sure he was in the room with me for the time being. I didn't trust my Dad with him yet. As far as I was concerned, it was just my son and me.

CHAPTER 21

I have learned that the power of a man's touch can be restorative as much as it can be infectious. I found myself thinking about Nathan and trying to figure out how things turned out the way it did. I can still feel him inside me at times. His affection, the way he held me when we made love and the passion; the passion was sometimes more than I could bear.

My mind drifts back to the night we conceived our son. We had not seen each other consistently in a few days and was yearning for each other. We decided to go to a drive-thru movie and then later, park by the lake nearby:

"SHIT!" Nate struggled with the lever. I was on top of him not caring what position he was trying to get into, I wanted him desperately and slid down on his shaft. "So. Good." He managed to utter.

Nate began to grab my breast, devouring them into his mouth. With each suck, the touch of his tongue intensified my soul. His hands intensely massaged me as they moved to the small of my back and back up to my neck. Nate had a way of caressing me. It was like he was molding me with his fingertips moving up and down my spine, assisting me in stroking his way through the walls of me. The same walls that I've allowed him to enter, however, it pleased him. Our rhythm was in sync, and he began to thrust harder and harder.

[knock, knock]

My heartfelt like it jumped out of my body and into my arms. Arms, which were covering my breast from the light that was shining into the car window. I reached between my legs and pulled Nate from inside me, and for a quick moment was pissed that I had to let him go for the moment. He felt so good.

"Oh my God, Oh my God!" I moved to the passenger side of the car and began putting back on my clothing or the lack thereof. I was in a panic. I couldn't find my underwear

anywhere. The windows were so foggy that the light was the only thing we could see.

"Roll down the window, please." the voice sounded like a trumpet.

"You straight?" Nate asked, making sure I was decent before rolling down the window. "Yeah, yeah." I didn't look too bad. I looked over my hair and face in the sun visor mirror while the window rolled down to a bright light shining directly in our faces.

"Officer." Nate greeted the man, his eyelids thinner now from trying to protect them from too much light.

"Yes, you need to vacate the premises. This is private property."

"Oh no problem, officer, thanks." I looked at Nate and then back at the officer the whole conversation hoping nothing went wrong. The cop leaned down a little to look over toward me.

"Ma'am." He tipped his hat. "Yall have a nice night."

I was so embarrassed I smiled awkwardly at the cop and leaned back into the seat. I believe the policeman knew we were having sex. He may have been standing off somewhere watching the whole time. All I know, I was glad that he let us go with a warning, and we were able to make it back home.

My father's house can feel somewhat cluttered but clean. It was filled to the rafters with books, old antiques. He would bring in so many old things, from different shops, from around town. Books were always a must in the house. He made me read all the time.

Mother would be so upset when Dad would come back home with yet another haul. This meant more dust to clean for my mother:

"You need to stop bringing that junk in this house, James." My mother stood by the front door of the house while my Dad and his

friend from next door helped him slide an old organ from the back of his truck into the house. He wanted me to learn to play but could not afford it or, in my mother's opinion, my father just didn't want to pay full price for one. Mama would say about my father that he'll be

"Too cheap to die."

She laughed a little. I looked at her in amazement at how she can find the humor in what she said. I thought it was the meanest thing you could say, but I guess they understood each other in their own way.

I stood looking out the window watching my father as he navigated his friend on how to move the organ. It was my first time looking at my father as a man and not just my father.

After moving the organ, he and his friend sat on the front porch with a beer. It was my first time seeing my Dad interact with anyone at the house. Father wasn't trustworthy of too many people and kept his distance from people. The man seemed friendly and genuine toward my father, so maybe he was different in his eyes.

Mom stayed in the kitchen or tended to other chores around the house while my Dad had company. I began to pick at the keys and listen to the different tempos and sounds. I clicked every button and every black and white key that was on the organ. Before I knew it, I was hooked and wanted to learn more.

"I see you still play?"

I gradually stopped playing to turn to my father, acknowledging him with a slight grin. I was in the middle of the second verse to "Amazing Grace" when Dad walked in on me traveling thru the past. He stood and watched as my hands passed from each key. "Couldn't sleep, or did I wake you?"

"A little bit of both." He scoffed and walked over to the chair in the living room with a glass of milk in his hand. He reached for an old magazine on the coffee table before he flopped back into the corner chair. This chair was his sanctuary, where you can find him at any given time when he was home.

"Well, I won't keep you." I was stopped in my tracks by a subtle sense of care.

"Wait, before you go..." the sincerity in his voice was foreign to my ears. "Clearly, there are some things that need to be said between the two of us. If you're going to be living here for however long you decide to stay, we might as well get it out in the open."

I did agree with this sentiment. I had so many questions about my past but was afraid of how it would damage my present. My future is uncertain, but I do believe I have a choice in molding myself toward what I think is a dream come true.

As I stood in the archway, I wondered if getting the answers, I needed, or just yearned for, would finally allow me to understand and love myself completely. Are the answers the glue to keep me together or the sledgehammer that will break me apart until I crumble.

I walked back into the living room and sat on the loveseat. The same loveseat I saw my mother's emotional breakdown take place. My father sat across from me in his chair, reading. I wasn't sure if he wanted me to start, or was I supposed to sit here like I was the 8-year-old little girl that wouldn't dare flinch while he was speaking. He looked up from the magazine he was reading and made a gesture with his thick eyebrows as to signal that he was ready for what was to proceed out of my mouth.

With all my might, I held back the very question that has haunted me for so long but the urge to know the unknown. I could not fight it off. I sat back on the loveseat. With a deep breath, the words seemed to flow. From my heart to my mind and then out of my mouth I uttered once again, "Are you my father?"

CHAPTER 22

I listened to my Dad as he told his side of the story about his marriage to my mother.

"She was raped, is what she said. I wanted to believe her, but something kept tugging at me to search more for the truth. She would never tell me who it was or a name. I would talk to our neighbor Mr. Deitrick about it; with him being a veteran as well, he understood what happens to women in the service, and it helped me thru a lot of the drama I was going thru with your mother. We were stationed together, ya know."

"Oh, I didn't know that!" I was surprised, and this was all new to me. We lived next to the Detricks practically all my life if my memory served me correctly.

I know how it is to have your body violated most terrifyingly. I could not imagine having to view a memento of the very moment of the scariest time of your life.

"Yeah. Then one day..." he paused for a moment. He had the look of despair on his face, and for a second, he seemed to have tears forming in the corner of his eyes. He struggled to continue.
"One day, what?" I inquired.

He swallowed hard and slid to the edge of his chair with his elbows on his knees. He seemed to contemplate his next move.

"Ya know what, forget it, it's getting late, and you've got a big day tomorrow."

Needless to say, I was a little disappointed. I wanted to know what caused my mother's breakdown or why she was like she was. I guess it was too painful for him to talk about, and I did not push him to relive his pain. The Lord above knows my struggle with dreams and flashbacks of what haunts me. I went over to my Dad and placed my hand on his back to comfort him.

"It's alright, I understand. Well, I'll see you in the morning, let me know if you need anything."

He took a deep breath and looked up at me with a slight grin. "Alright, goodnight, dear."

CHAPTER 23

WHAT ABOUT DENISE?

I was always on-the-go. I was determined to be the best, and the best is what I shall be. Is that too boastful? Should I not chase success? What else is there? Maybe I've worked so much that I forgot about the one thing that everyone yearns for. We wake up in the middle of the night, hoping that it's still out there. Hoping that it hasn't forgotten about you. You denounce it from time to time that it even exists, but at the same time, it can make you angry waiting around for it. I admit I have tried giving up on it. But we know better, and without it, we would be lost, still searching, looking for something or someone to love and for them to love you back.

"This is highly inappropriate. I have to ask you to leave."

Another "patient" who has become attached and cannot let go. "No, I didn't mean anything by it, it's just that..."

"I know what you meant, Mr. Martez but, that's where I draw the line, and we must end our session for today." I stood for him to get the hint that it was time to go. I usually would give my patients a slight smile of reassurance that all will be well, but not this time.

You see, Mr. Martez is the type that feels he is entitled to any woman he sees just because he may say something beautiful or give a compliment. Sometimes he doesn't consider his surroundings, and his reality is just a figment of the big picture. For the tenth time, I had to advise him of his annoying advances. I was fed up.

I guided him toward the door. He looked disappointed, of what, I'm not sure, but I hope he can figure it out. "I swear, I didn't mean to offend you. It's just that…" he had that sexy smirk he usually would give. I was not falling for it. Of course, the man was fine but, not today.

"Diane, can you take care of Mr. Martez for me?" She shook her head in agreement with the situation. I walked back to my office, feeling the glare of his eyes on my behind as I opened the door.

"Ok, Mr. Martez, I have some paperwork for you to sign, right…" I can hear Diane speaking as I closed the door behind me and leaned backward to take a deep breath. The sight of that man for the past four months has been torture.

Mr. Martez, or should I say Anthony is just my type. He reminds me of a past love I once knew but in a different form. It would be disastrous, and I promised myself to stick to my oath of never, NEVER dating patients.

The buzzer sounded from Diane's desk, and my nerves became on edge as I hoped there was not a problem with Anthony again. "You have another visitor; a Nathan Carter is requesting to see you?"

My heart dropped the moment I heard her speak the name. It felt like someone decided to reach down in the deep parts of my heart and scoop out the locked away pain that I dreadfully did not want to revisit at this time. "Can you ask him to wait, please?"

"Sure."

I sat in my desk chair, took and deep breath. "Ugh!!!" I flopped my head down on my desk, leaning on my arms as I tried to gain the strength to deal with the upcoming battle of resistance.
No matter where you are in life, no matter what you think you can escape, I know for sure love is always around the corner in some form or another. Today, I guess, was the day for me to deal or fold.
I lifted my head and looked over to the full-length mirror in the corner. I ran over and started to fix my hair and clothing to look presentable on the outside, at least. I looked at myself and gave myself a look of strength.

"I will not be tempted by his starry green eyes. I will not be mesmerized by his charisma."

[KNOCK][KNOCK]

Diane knocked on the door before I could finish going down the list things I will not do or try to.

"Come in."

"Uh, yes. Your guest is waiting." She was standing by the door with her head in only. I signaled for her to come in, and she closed the door behind her. Diane was not only my secretary but a friend. She ran the staffing thru her agency for my practice.

"I know! What does Nathan want, what did he say?"

"Nothing. Only that he needed to see you about an appointment." She looked at me with concern.

"Girl, I couldn't be you." She laughed a little as she walked back to the door to stall. She knew exactly what to do.

Diane gave me three more minutes to get myself together. {buzz}

"Yes?" I answered as coldly as possible. I knew he could hear me. "Send him in."

Another five minutes past. *"Good job Diane,"* I said to myself. I was standing in front of the door, so I can be the first thing he sees. But then I thought to just sit at my desk. I do not want him to think I had the time. After all, he did just pop up in the middle of nowhere, expecting me to stop everything I'm doing without respecting my schedule.

"Yeah, the desk."

I went toward the desk and sat down and adjusted my seating. I heard the door began to open. The handle moved back and forth as if someone had problems getting in. The door slowly opened.

"Thank you."

Even after all these years, his voice still sounded the same. It immediately took me back to a time where everything was imperfectly perfect, and there was no care in the world for me that would affect it. I looked up, and there they were, those green eyes that would always breathe life in me each time I was able to gaze upon them. The renewal of his energy and mine was refreshing, and I was thirsty.

"Denise."

CHAPTER 24

Having someone around is a necessity for my security and way of life. Having someone to love and them loving you in abundance keeps me alive and hopeful. To hear his voice was a relief. I thought David had gone back home by now, but he decided to stay a little longer.

"How are you today?" David had a swank persona that was quite appealing.

He had called to let me know that he stayed an extra day and wanted to take Nate Jr and me out to the park for lunch. Naturally, I accepted. I needed a breath of fresh air because being back home was bringing back too many memories that I couldn't focus on this moment in my life.

"Taking it one day at a time." I sighed as I leaned against the kitchen wall. This was the same wall I would run into each time the phone would ring when I thought James would be calling me.

"I appreciate this."

"Oh, it's no problem, I miss you." David's compassion sounded like the soundtrack to my heart.

"I hope my buddy is excited."

"He truly is and getting better each day."

"It's a miracle." David's enthusiasm toward Nathan Jr's breakthrough was such an alleviation of my spirit.

We met David at the same park where I was raped by Lewis years ago. It was walking distance from the house, so I decided to take a stroll so I can talk to Junior more. He was starting to form complete sentences, and it felt as if I had awakened to a whole new world of his. Our minds were in sync.

Chills traveled up my spine as I remembered the night in my head, passing across the green grass, staring at the concreted area where the car was parked. I wondered if anyone saw us that night, and I never told a soul about what happened to me. I'm glad I was able to get out and survive physically, but the mental damage is another.

I wanted David to be that continuing relief in my life, but I wasn't sure if I was strong enough for the commitment he wanted. Yes, the heart can be deceitful and who it belongs to matters. An attachment can be so powerful to where you can no longer hold on to the past. You MUST move forward. As far as I was concerned, I was through with men. I wanted to truly regain who I indeed was and who I am supposed to be but being around him felt right.

We approached where David was placing the lunch items on the picnic table. I was usually not fond of picnics. The flies and heat can be a damper in the summertime but, today was different. There were not any annoying bugs or the sting you feel from the sun beaming down on your body. Autumn had finally fallen upon us, and at this moment, I found myself doing the same with David. Then, why does my mind continue to lie in telling me what my heart is feeling isn't real?

"Hey, come on over, sit." He gestured.

He took Junior's hand and placed him on the side of the benched table where I had taken a seat. I wanted to hug him, but I decided to keep it platonic as possible. Honestly, I was waiting for him to make the first move. If he did care enough to tell me how he felt, he would. I didn't want to rush into anything as I was still vulnerable from divorcing Nathan.

I have a fear of eventually being rejected and hated by David due to my past. It seems that's how all my relationships ended. Not having love continuously in my life was my fate, but I refuse to think this is true.

The last day I lived with my husband was one of the most dreadful times of my life. I never thought Nathan and I would have split. Our family was surprised by the news, and it brought turmoil on top of the bitterness surrounding us:

"I don't want to be married anymore, Marissa!"

"Well, fine. I can't make you stay. You got your nerve."

After all the blows I took. After having his son. The back and forth, in and out of the house and sometimes not coming home antics by Nathan, he decides to abandon us. He was becoming unbearable. He continuously pushed me further and further away from him as if he were purposely trying to get me to end the marriage.

Yes, I cheated. I confessed this sin to him after our divorce. If I had told him the truth, then he probably would have done more than give me another black eye. But I had to speak this truth so that I may move on. I asked God to forgive me each day for this terrible thing, and I believe I was forgiven, but I had to forgive myself.

During the time that our marriage was in turmoil, I found pictures of him and Denise.

They were buried at the bottom of our closet under the wooden planks. This is the moment I decided I had had enough and decided to give him a taste of his own medicine:

"What are these, Nathan?" An explanation was due, and I was determined to get one. "Are you still seeing her?"

"No, Marissa. All we did was take a picture."

"Looked like more than a picture to me. So, your hand had to touch her ass like that?" Who did he think he was trying to fool? The way she was sitting in my husband's lap, it seemed, she had already taken more than just a picture.

I threw the photographs at him.

"Fuck it!"

I had been hurt for the last time and was in the mood to lash out. So, to avoid another violent ordeal, I walked off with my hands up in the air, and instead of turning it over to God, I decided to be vengeful.

CHAPTER 25

"It was nice seeing you again, Marissa."

David and I were outside of my fathers' house catching up a bit. From the day we met until now, he has grown drastically. A man is what I saw, it was different from what I was used to. Seeing how he could love scared me. Why I couldn't honor him back with the same feelings was beyond my understanding. Maybe he was here to replenish the love that Nathan took away from me. You must give respect to receive it, but love is different. Love is just what it is, no questions ask, no conditions attached.

I smiled as sweetly as I could in response to his kind words. I was fond of David, but not in love. His type of love, the way he knew exactly what I needed when I needed it, wasn't what I was used to. Our connection was overpowering, and the desire to be closer had taken over.

"Good to see you too, and thanks for inviting us, David. I needed to get out." I sighed deeply and looked out toward the street, watching a car go by.

"So, what are you going to do? Are you staying permanently?" he seemed hesitant with his words. I knew what he wanted to know, and I was not ready to discuss it yet.

"I'm not sure, David." I was confused, and I'm sure he could understand that. He is persistent but reasonable.

"Look, Marissa." He straightened up a little as if he were preparing for Sunday School. "I know the way I came to you concerning your husband was a bit off."

"Ya think?"

He smirked slightly. "I deserve that."

"You scared the shit out of me?"

"You wouldn't return any of my calls, so I had to get your attention somehow. I'm sorry, please forgive me."

I thought he had forgotten about me by then anyway. He was so angry at me for choosing Nathan. I assumed he was done with me, even as a friend. "No, you're right. I purposely ignored your calls in hopes that you would get the idea that..."

"That what?"

I scoffed at the thought that I was no longer with Nathan. "Never mind, it's not important anymore."

CHAPTER 26

The birth of Nathan Carter Jr was a precious thing to witness in the glory of the Most High. I felt he was a gift from above that was given to me so that I may know how to love. So, I named him Nathan, meaning YHWH has given. He is what old folks would say a little touched. I see him as a boy that takes in the world a little differently than most. Junior is absolutely remarkable. Sometimes, in the way he communicates, he unlocks my mind to another dimension. Insightfully as it is, I still doubt myself as a mother.

It was Juniors' 6th birthday. I wanted to keep him home, but when dealing with children who need the consistency as he does, it was best to let him go on to school before celebrating. His bus pulled up right on schedule. The look in my son's eyes when he saw his father standing next to me was beyond imaginable. Nathan has been great at spending time with our son and being there for him. At times, it can be too much for

Junior to bear with his father living in another state.

A smile of joy came over my face as I watched Junior walk to get off the bus. He had to wait a moment and started to become unglued emotionally. Being patient can be exceedingly difficult for him to endure. He leaned over the bus drivers' seat with his head down buried in his hands. While she tried to let him know he could come to us, it was too late; Junior was already in his whirlwind. In his emotional state, the anticipation of hugging his father became overwhelming, and to stop him for even one second was like someone hit him with a hammer. Love is effectual.

We were finally able to get Junior off the bus, but he was frantic. I had his arm so he would not lose his balance as he began to mimic someone with the Holy Ghost that was about to pass out from being slain in the spirit.

"Oh, c'mon Junior. You know better." His fathers' words did not absorb within his understanding.

Junior somehow got away from me and took off so fast I lost the grip I had on him.

"JUNIOR!"

I yelled and yelled for him to stop. I saw him go around to the back of the bus as I ran with all my might to stop him. I heard Nathan Sr in the background, and everything became surreal as if I were caught up in a dream.

"STOP, JUNIOR STOP!"

The sound of tires screeching was so loud it felt as though it burst my eardrum. Junior looked directly in the path of the oncoming car. My heart dropped as I knew in my heart that this was the last time, I was going to see my child alive. I knew this was the last time I would get to see his sweet smile as I did each morning when I would wake him up to start his day. The sound of gasping was in the air, as everyone anticipated the inevitable, seem to make time stop. My heart pumped with the hope of a miracle from above. Before I knew it, Nate quickly grabbed him by the top of his pants. He spanned him around so fast that he almost lost his balance, but he had Junior.

I fell to my knees as the burden of losing my son today was lifted. I've never felt so helpless in my life. As I looked up to look for Junior so I could hold him, I saw Nathan pacing with him in his arms. The realization of losing our son had settled in, and knowing Nathan, his mind was racing in every direction.

Days like this help remind us that there are more things in life far more important than ourselves.

CHAPTER 27

Nathan came back to get Nathan Jr for the summer. I was lost without my seed. The time alone forced me to deal with myself, and it wasn't pretty. I thought I was going to go insane.

****

The following episodes are
the emotions I have felt toward my birth mother.
They are inspired by true events
And were written to fit the format of this story.
****

I decided to add this portion for you,
my reader,
to experience a deeper part of me.

Episode I

Here begins another story, another trial, another tribulation of the ups and downs of the relationship I have with my mother. The way you are guided to grow up in life can come in various ways. Everyone is not fated to be brought up in the illusion-based world that is peddled to us each day. My family was not different from any other dysfunctional family. My mother may have had her own problems with being Mrs. Orville, but those same issues influenced me more than what some textbook or some mind programming tool can ever do.

My mother was the eldest of twelve. She grew up in a household that was missing love for the bulk of her childhood. She would get beaten by her mother; her brothers would mistreat her; it was a traumatizing time. Ever since her father left, life had turned completely upside down, and everything went straight to hell. I know you want to speculate that her father was the one that held the family together, you may want to try and comprehend what kind of a man would desert a woman with twelve children. He had no choice; it was either stay and perish or flee and exist:

"You're lying!" my mother's face was inflated from the tears and the unbelievable

slap she just suffered at my grandmother's hand.

Mother just unveiled her darkest secret to her mother, and no compassion was given. From the one person she thought would understand, the burn on her face told a different tale. Something like this should not happen, mainly, from one family member to another, but it happens all the time. The unsettling life it can bring to an adolescent's existence can be not only damaging emotionally but mentally as well. I believe this is where the mental damage originated with my mother.

"Why would I lie?"

"You just shut up, ya hear me, just shut up!"

My grandfather had appeared in my mother's room one night and raped her. My grandmother believed that she lured him, and he couldn't help himself. "Your whorish tendencies devised this whole mess. This whole mess."

There was no way that my grandmother was going to accept that her husband, of almost twenty years, would do such a foul and atrocious act.

"Of course, mama, it's always my fault. You will never want to see things for what they truly are. Go on ahead! Continue to exist in that confined world of yours. Do you think the people down at the church don't know who Daddy is?" With tears in her eyes, this was the moment my mother decided to not take any more of the manipulation and abuse.

"You get out of my house, and I mean right now!" These were the last words my mother had ever heard her mother speak to her. The discontentment between the two of them has been going on for years, and so has the abuse.

My mother once told me she thought she would be better off if she didn't have parents. She would preferably have been carried down to earth and raised by

wolves. *"At least they protect their young,"*
she would say.

I used to judge my mother as I grew older.
Her decision to leave me with my Dad when
I was younger; the lies about who my father
is. These were just a few of the experiences
with my mother that created a distance
between us. One day I found out the truth
about my mother's erratic behavior:

"Mom."

"Oh, hey, honey!" I observed my mother
covered in paint. It was three in the
morning, and the sounds coming from my
mother's bedroom awaken me. I'm not sure
who she was talking to, but the conversation
was so compelling that she did not see me
walk in. The room was covered and
scattered of canvases of different sizes. The
paintings of vibrant colors intertwined so
beautifully. There was never a picture of a
specific object or theme. Everything was
abstract.

I walked further into the room, looking around in amazement of all the paintings. My mother stood in the middle of the room, looking exhausted. "I guess I got a little carried away," she said. Her voice was the tone of embarrassment.

I discovered a part of her that was hidden. It was not too long after I moved in with my mom that I found out about her struggle with being bipolar.

Episode II

Life is not easy. It is a constant daily battle. Tribulations, like sickness and failure, can crush our spirits. False values and easy promises can entice us and even destroy our souls. So, we ask God to keep us from failing these trials when we are tested, to help teach us the right thing to do. We also ask for deliverance from the evils and temptations which await us in life.

My mother's episodes would come and go, but at the end of the day, she was my mother, and I loved her. I remember a time when she and my father were arguing. I'm not sure what the conversation was about, but the way my father threw my mother against the heater, I was sure she was dead. I screamed at the top of my lungs:

"MOMMY!"

I ran over to aide my mother, who seemed to have the wind knock out of her. She had slid down to the floor from the impact, and I tried to catch her before she fell on the floor. "Mom." Tears were streaming down my eyes as I lifted her head to look upon her face. She looked tired and worn as if she's been in battle all day.

"Go back to your room." My father was walking toward us. For a moment, I did see a look of regret in his face. I believe him realizing my presence in the room brought him back to reality. When my mother would be detached from reality, I think he would take that journey with her and lose himself in the process. He was fed up, but in my view, that was no excuse.

I put my arms around her, bringing her close as he approached. "No, leave her alone."

"It's okay, baby, go on." She could barely get her words out as she coughed a little. She kissed me on the side of my head and patted me on my back for reassurance, but it wasn't enough for me. Seeing her this way was troubling and heartbreaking; I began to tremble.

My mother made her way to her feet as she guided me to mine. She hugged me tight and began to walk me back to my room. "Just let her be. Its late," father said.

I looked up at my mothers' face, and there was no expression as she led me to my room. My five-year-old mind could not really comprehend what was really going on at the time. All I know is that I started to feel uneasy.

"Mommy, I'm thirsty." She stopped immediately. I'm not sure what was going on

in her mind, she looked sick but not physically.

"Jean. Let her go." My father approached slowly and leaned out his hand to take mine. My mother had a grip on my arm that was starting to dig thru my skin. She was hurting me. I do not believe she meant to, but the intensity of her strength was beginning to become unbearable.

"NO, SHE'S MINE." Mother shouted so loudly; I was sure the neighbors were awakened. By now, my mother had my back against her and was holding me captive. She would not let me go.

"Jean, please. Stop this. You're not well." My father begged, pleading with her. I looked over to my right and saw a bloody knife on the floor, and at that moment, I realized the blood dripping from my fathers' arm.

I wanted to help my mother. I wanted the episodes of detachment that would come and go to be completely erased from her life.

She was starting to be a danger to not only herself, but to others as well. I realized I had just walked in the middle of my father defending himself from my mother rather than just beating her.

Episode III

The ambulance came for my mother but did not take her away to a hospital. I stood in the doorway and watched them take her as if she were a criminal more so than a patient. My mother turned and looked at me with uncertainty, but I didn't judge her. When you feel trapped, the most natural thing to do is to seek out what will set you free.

What had my mother in bondage, I was not sure of but, I would spend the rest of my life trying to avoid it. Being afraid of turning into my mother has been a conquest not because I thought she was a horrible person, but I wanted to live the way I'm sure she dreamed of living.
As my mother was placed in the white van, her picture-perfect face seemed to look traced upon the window, which reflected

from the sun. I thought back to happier times when her face used to be covered with smiles that would cover the earth for miles as if she were the reason there was light in the world.

"Okay, we are done."

She held up the stained-glass canvas we just completed together. It reminded me of the glass in the window of the church that was down the street. We attended service some Sundays, and Daddy would sometimes come as well. I loved spending time with my mother. She was a pure delight. My admiration for her would fill my heart. I had hoped to be a direct replica of her. She was my muse of all things in life; my everything.

"Ooo, pretty, Mommy!" I smiled as bright as I could. I felt my cheeks becoming weak, but I could not stop. It was the happiest day of my life, and I did not want it to end.

"What do you want to do next? Oh, I know, go get your dolls, and we can make little clothes and do their hair."

I got up from the side of the glass coffee table and ran to my room. I stopped in the middle of the room, breathing heavily from excitement and started scanning the place for the perfect combination of dolls to play with. I had a variety of them, some with short hair; long. Some were of different ethnicity and races. My mother wanted to show me not only is being black is beautiful but that all women are beautiful, and it was okay to see the beauty in that way. I started to pick up the dolls I wanted. One was a "Cabbage Patch" doll that I loved dearly. It was the first African American doll that I had, and I loved it so much that some of her hair started to come out from combing it constantly. But I didn't care, I snatched her up from the floor where she laid and placed her in my arms along with a few others I wanted to play with.

"Here, Mom, let's play with these." I turned to see my mom standing in the doorway of my room, watching as I selected my favorites. She had a smile on her face that

would remove any negative energy a person may have inside them.

"Alright, get your hair box too."

I picked up the box, and we walked back to the living room area where we stained the glass we made. Mom had picked up most of the art supplies we used and cleared the glass coffee table to make room for our next project. I placed the dolls and my hair box on the table and opened it to take out the barrettes and ribbons we were going to use.

"Where's the brush, dear?"

"On my dresser in my room, I'll go get it." I jumped up so fast my mother became startled a little. I was excited. She was having one of her "good days."

"Okay but be careful now."

I ran back to my room and swooped the brush from my dresser as fast as I could. My fast pace was due to the fact I never knew when my mother would snap out of the

"happy place" she was in. I would savor each moment before she would or if when she would be back to the dark sadness that would suddenly overcome her.
"Here, Momma!" As I was running back, I failed to see the extension cord that helps energize the stereo system that was in the room. I loved to see them dance in the middle of the living room and embrace each other in love. I would stand at the doorway, with my head rested against the wall and watch them, hoping that I would one day experience that same feeling with someone. Being in-love seemed so natural to me at the time, but as I grew up, I realized it's one of the hardest things to do.

My foot hit the cord, and I tripped forward. "Oh, no, Marissa!" I heard my mom yell out as I fell. I used my left hand to break my fall by grabbing the coffee table. I thought I was okay until I stood back up and look at my hand. I had cut the side of it deeply. Blood was oozing out of it, and I saw, what I thought was a bone, go in and out of it.

I wailed in agony.

I had never felt so alone than when the day my mother left. Her presence was the reason I felt that my life would have a happy ending. While she was gone, my fathers' anger and resentment toward her needed a place to reside. His inability to take it out on her created an abusive monster, and it was damaging to my emotional and mental well-being. I began to die inside each day with every harsh word and mean look. I needed refuge, an escape from the turmoil.

My heart would ache at the thought of my mother because I missed her terribly. I longed for her touch, to see her smile just once more so that I may be able to continue. I laid in my bed that night with tears in my eyes. I cried because of the unknown life ahead. I needed to know if I would see my mother again to shed a glimpse of the hope I needed so badly. I was miserable. My bedroom light came on, and I was startled.

"Make sure your alarm is set to wake up on time. We have to go get your mother in the morning." My dad was standing in the doorway as I sat up to listen to his instruction. The look he had on his face was of disappointment. He looked tired and fed up, but I didn't care. He turned the life off and slammed the door. My misery turned into comfortability, knowing that joy would be coming in the morning.

*"Delight yourself in the Lord and
He will give you the desires of your heart."
~Psalm 37:4~*

Episode IV

The morning seemed odd. No birds were chirping, and I didn't smell the scent of breakfast and love in the air. The thickness of the unsettling atmosphere in the house seemed to way me down, but I got up out of bed anyway. I walked in the kitchen, and after taking the first step, I knew there had been a spirit of confusion within our home. My goal was to walk over to the laundry area to get a clean top out of the dryer for school. The kitchen was pitch black, and I could not see a thing. I felt a squishy substance between my toes with each step and was unsure of what it was. The smell was unbearable. I finally was able to flip the switch to see my surroundings, and all the food we had in the house was dumped on the floor of the kitchen. It was a pigsty, and I could barely move about without almost slipping and falling.

"Who would do such a thing, and why?" I thought to myself as I made my way out. There was food residue left on the living room carpet from me walking back to my room. I went into the bathroom to wash my feet in the tub. My spirit was numb to the chaos around me currently. My mothers' behavior was of the norm. I got dressed for school and headed out the door. Once I was out of the house, I took in the fresh air. I felt free as a slave that had been in bondage for four hundred years.

CHAPTER 28

The hardest truth was I never felt lonely in my life, only afraid of who I was when I was alone and not with a man. Nathan Jr was away for the summer, and I started to pick myself apart. Without my son, I was so insecure and, I felt so unneeded and without purpose. As a woman, that can be hard to grasp. The Bible speaks of being a 'help meet' to a man, but I'm sure it's so much more that comes with being a female than just being with a man.

And the Lord God said,
"It is not good that the man should be alone;
I will make him an help meet for him."
~Genesis 2:18~

When my son was away with his father, I took a step back out of my own picture that I imagined my life to be. My desire to better myself started to take over me each day as I would look in the mirror. The picture in my head sometimes blinded me from my own existence.

I still desired to be loved, and like any other mother, I wanted my child to be safe. I had a desire to be understood, and to gain the peace that you receive whether times were good or bad. I wanted to be set free of the troubles that this world can bring living within it.

"I aim to detour my life in the direction of my own destiny, not my mothers'."

I repeated this phrase in the mirror over and over each morning. Perhaps, it was fear of inheriting my mother's illness, or it was my way of drowning out the truth that in many ways, I was just like her. I understood her struggles, but she had her way of coping, and I had mine. I decided to choose love.

CHAPTER 29

Spending one on one time with David, built a fondness, not only for myself but him as well. I grew more attached to the way he would smirk at my quirky jokes. I became more affectionate of the way he would allow me to lean back on his chest and jabber on as he rubbed my head and pretended to listen. I grew more captivated by the way he would always snack right before dinner. I became more loving about how impatient he can be. He was enchanting.

We've been on a daily routine of seeing each other. David was very introverted, and from the first glance of him, he would appear "peculiar" to some, but I did not mind that. He was just a tranquil man, who listened more than he spoke, but when he did have something to say, watch out he'll have you either angrier than you've ever been or before you know it, you'll be looking for your panties in the morning. I had to get out of my father's house and get my own place, so, with David's guidance, I was able to obtain employment and finally move out with my son.

"You alright?"

Months had passed since we had the chance to go out. We would jump at every opportunity to be together. His thoughtfulness in asking made me feel tender. He knew he could get a little rough when his concupiscence is turned all the way up during it.

"I'll survive."

Breathing heavily while I adjusted the covers, David got up. His silhouette was divine. He reached for the water pitcher that was on his terrace. The moonlight resembled a kiss upon his statue in every place conceivable.

"You're right, you'll survive." He said jokingly.

David had a way with words that I valued. His quirkiness can be unusual. To most, what is a red flag, is not to me; he's a little deeper than that. I love listening to him even though he is introverted, private, a lover of beautiful things, but not gaudy.

His apartment is considered industrial with a few rustic touches. A professor would live here, with all the books accumulated around, but placed strategically to incorporate the feeling of a lounge library. David was well-read. I, on the other hand, am more of a vivid observer. My extroverted side exceeds more than it should sometimes.

"Must you be an A-HOLE at every possible moment you get to be?"

I clutched his neck and tickled him as he laid back onto my unapologetically bare body chilled from the warm breeze coming thru the sliding doors. Warmth transfused within my skin from him, and I felt innate.

"Only the moments that count, like this." He began to kiss my body with his soft lips.

These lips were created in the potters' house. The fullness of each embrace on my body felt like a full lip massage. They would butterfly out as he cuffed my breast and used them to caress my nipples. The sexiness that David possessed while in the bedroom would take over me, and he was able to do whatever he pleased at any time. Out of the bedroom, you would not know who he was. It was enthralling.

I moaned in satisfaction of him suckling the fruit of my garden. He filled his belly with it and continued sinfully as if it were forbidden. With every embrace, I felt my womb create a light as it woke up to the welcoming of his tongue. He had his entire face between my legs going up, down, and sideways. He covered every inch of my lower body until I exploded. I arched my back and lifted myself on my toes. I had to hold onto the headboard to keep from sliding to the foot of the bed directly on David's face, which I ultimately think that is where he was going. A firm grip around my waist was his aim. There was no escaping this transcendence into another dimension. He knew exactly where to lick, where to touch, how hard to punch it to bring me to the right speed to where I was headed.

"Ah! Ah!"

I thought Nathan knew my body. David came along and took his time and studied my physique. He watched what made my body tick. He treated our time together with such attention. I have never had an attraction to develop for someone like this before. Each day grew better than the next. He and Nathan Jr seemed to get along as well. Nate does not know that I'm seeing David, and I would like to keep it that way, but the more David and I get closer, it's hard to keep him and Nate from stumbling into each other. Nate decided to move back after the divorce to be closer to our son. He spends every other weekend with Junior, which does give me a break with handling him.

David spent the night, and Nathan brought Junior over a day earlier than expected without any warning. I was trying to figure out what happened the night before so much it drove me into a frenzy. All I know, I heard banging at the front door, and it had to be stopped.

"Hey, Dave, wake up."

I tugged at his arms to wake him. I was trying to imagine who would be at the door this time of the morning.

"Somebody's at the door."

I got out of bed and found my house shoes. I walked over to the window that looked directly down toward my front door.

"What in the wor-?"

I saw Junior standing outside with his overnight bag in hand and Nathan standing next to him, one hand in his pocket. He took his left hand and rubbed the top of Junior's head.

"Dave!" I put a little snap in my voice to wake him up.

He shifted a little, and his dark-brown sugar skin reflected a ray of the sun against the white sheets that were barely covering him. He was glorious.

"Yes, Marissa." I can hear the exhaustion in his voice.

He struggled to turn over and sit up to investigate what was so urgent to wake him from his slumber.

"Nate. He's outside."
"Ok. Well, go open the door, or do you want me to?" David said.

His suggested unthoroughly thought out act represented the fear of what I have been avoiding ever since Nate moved back. I could not see a positive outcome of David and Nathan reuniting under these circumstances.

"Are you crazy? He knows nothing of us being together and given the two of you and the history behind that, I don't think that's a good idea."

I reluctantly went downstairs to greet the unknown behind my door. I hope nothing was wrong with Junior, I was under enough pressure as it is. Approaching the door, I felt a huge lump in my chest that seems to not pass thru. I was not sure of the outcome of this unplanned event, and I begin to panic. I tend to let my thoughts run away with me at times, and this brings on my anxiety.

"Breathe," I told myself as I approached the door and finally turned the handle.

The last time Nathan and I were in this position was when he came back home, apologizing when I kicked him out. Nathan's words plucked at my heart, I fell in his trap and played his song. Before I knew it, he had found his way back into my garden, tasting every juice of the fruits that were being offered to him, again:

"I missed you, baby!" Nathan grabbed my ass with an unrelenting grip as he would thrust in and out as slow but hard as he

could. I thought my hip was going to break, but admittedly it did feel good.

"Ah!" I was finally able to speak after having my face shoved in the pillow as he slapped my ass. I could still feel the vibration from the tingle he left from his handprint stamp of approval. Nathan knew how to bring me to my destination in so many ways, and the barbaric way he handled me in the bedroom turned me on.

My body shivered and shook as I surrendered to the submission of his love inside of me. I felt rejuvenated. I thought that this time would be different. He screwed me so good you could not tell me without a shadow of a doubt that this man loved me.

CHAPTER 30

"What did you say?" I rubbed Juniors' head.

"Nothing."

"Slow down when you're chewing, you may choke?"

He began to pick at his pizza some more. "It's hot."

"Hot?"
"Yep!"

Junior seemed to be starving. "Did he eat yet?"

Pointing my questioning toward Nathan. Nathan answered with his usual smug face, but I did not care. "Yeah, he's a growing boy. What do you expect?"

"I'm just saying, he seemed to act as though this was his first meal in; I don't know how long," I exclaimed.

"I don't have time for this."

Nathan stood up from the breakfast table, where he was watching Junior eat. I was hoping that David didn't get alarmed and come downstairs. The roof began to creak.

"What's that?" Nathan looked toward the sky but not to give all praises to the Most High.

"Uh, probably the house settling. You know these old houses." I lied.

"You wanted this house, not me." He began to start in, but I was not interested so, I interrupted.

"Well, yeah, okay. Were you on your way out?"

"Damn! What's up with you today?" He looked at me with suspicion more than concern.

I just needed him to leave. I was pissed about him showing up without calling or giving me a heads up but, I was willing to set that aside and forfeit that battle to prevent a war.

"Nothing. I am just not feeling well. That's all."

"Well, alright, I'll get out of your hair." He gave Junior a kiss on the forehead. "See you later, son, love you."

I felt more and more relieved, the closer he got to the door. I heard another creak from upstairs, and Nathan stopped and turned to look up again.

"You sure that's the house settling?"

"Yeah, I'm sure of it." I nodded, trying to paint with my mind the most innocent face that I could display.

You could play music to the beat of my heart. The ups and downs began to race against each other, and my stomach began to turn. Pretending not to show how nervous I felt, every organ inside of me began performing its own function, and I passed gas.

"Alright, I'm out."

"Okay, see you next week."

"Bye, Daddy." Junior belted out from the breakfast table.

{I hope you're smiling, as I was when I wrote it}

The feeling I felt was of fear. I realized I was being controlled. This was my house, my life, and he was only a part of it thru our son. Whom I choose to love was not of his concern. The thoughts racing thru my head were only inches away from exiting my mouth. The door closed behind him, and he was halfway to his car once I realized the opportunity had passed. All was left was his scent in the air, creating the sweetest musk that can be cultivated for a man. He smelled as Adam, in the beginning, my beginning and now my end.

CHAPTER 31

"See, that wasn't so bad. Now, was it?"

I turned to see David dressed and standing at the other end of the foyer. A sense of peace came over me, hearing his voice. Fear had been laid to rest, and love had moved in. I felt I could take on all my adversities and conquer them. He had a smile that could blind you with the meekness of a lamb. The possession of light grabbed my entire heart, and the shine warmed it as he pulled me closer into the stout build that gave me security. I felt safe and cherished for the first time.

I took a deep breath and hugged David so tight. I seemed to be caught up in a whirlwind, and I did not have a care in the world. Truth be told, I had fallen in love with David and didn't realize it until now. He had given up a lot for me and has been here in my time of need.

We continued to embrace each other without saying a word. We always knew what to say and what not to say to each other, words seemed to not matter.

"All Done."

We both laughed a little as our distant thoughts were brought back to reality. Junior had finished his lunch and was ready to get into something more interesting.

"Alright, lets clean up." I started helping Junior with his dishes.

David sat at the end of the counter. I did not want to talk about Nathan; it was too uncomfortable. I wanted to stay in the rapture, safe, and sound.

"So, my love." He said so sweetly.

"Yes." I sighed a little dreading the conversation that was in its infant stages.

"You need to tell him, honestly."

CHAPTER 32

Hate is an emotion that I loathe to enter my spirit, but for some reason or some way, it found its way into my heart. Love had disappeared along with reasoning. Love cannot remain when animosity, anger, and resentment are taking up space in the dwelling where friendship, kindness, and delight should be present.

Denise and I bumped heads a long time ago when we were kids and never reconciled or entertained each other. She was the type of person I did not attract in my life. Somehow, animosity was always present, I stayed out of her way. From my recollection, she was rude and acted like the world owed her something. It was right before recess. I had my foot on the leg of my friends' chair when she passed and bumped it. At first, I thought it was an accident until I noticed she walked off without acknowledging that she hit my leg:

"Ouch! Excuse you!?"

She looked back at me as if I dared to address her. "Okay. You're excused."

Her eye roll burned a hole in my soul, and I wanted revenge. I was tired of being a pushover, someone that nobody would care about if I would disappear off the face of the earth. I was tired of my feelings, not being respected.

"Well, watch where you're going, your excuse or not." I was furious. She continued her merry way along with Leah, another confused soul I grew up with.

We sat thru school, completing more work exercises in class. Denise's rudeness was still on my mind, and I was determined to humble her. After we turned in our handwriting lessons, it was time to go out to recess. I had made up in my mind to let it go and not give it another thought, but as soon as my little crew and I walked over to our area that we played each day, guess who was there taking over the territory:

 "I don't need permission," Denise replied with a side-eye and a neck roll. She seemed to keep an attitude for one reason or another.

"Well, this is our area; always been since the first grade, and we don't know you, so you have to move." I gave her the same amount of sass she gave me. An eye-for-an-eye.

"I'm not goin' nowhere."

"Yes, you are!" It was not that serious to me at this point, I was having fun with her. I'm not the bullying type, but sometimes it feels good to be on the other side of the river for a change.

"Whatever!!" She fanned me away with her hand to really let me know that she was not in the least worried about my mannerisms and head movements.
I had to up the intensity and, I saw James overlooking afar off. Suddenly I grabbed her plait and tugged as hard as I could. Before I knew it, I found myself in the middle of the

playground, trying to hold on to the kung-Fu grip I had on this little hussy's hair.

"Let her go, Marissa!!" I was on the ground from a push that seemed to come with its own gush of wind. "You're always trying to boss people around; she can sit where she wants!"

I can hear the laughter of the other kids on the playground. My underwear was exposed from falling on the ground, and my dress, covered in the playground dirt, made it harder to see when the wind blew it above my head. I was embarrassed and had started to regret my decision to not take the high road.

After that day, I would see Denise in the halls or out in the neighborhood in passing, but I never had any interest in getting to know her any better than I did. I saw all I needed to see within that first meeting. She was an absent-minded, self-centered cunt that did not care about anyone else but herself and her perseverance. The nerve of obtaining what she decided to let go a long time ago was very bold. But, again, why did I have to be the landfill, once again. Her selfishness changed my entire life.

I decided to meet with Denise. Talking to her and getting some questions answered might help me get Nathan out of my system. Going any further in my relationship with David was important to me. Until I could let go of all my anger about my past marriage, I couldn't see David and me together. The resentment I held against this woman was unhealthy. A need to be sifted thru to get to the root is how I will live free.

I gazed out the window of the coffee shop. The sky was silver with just a peek of the sun shining as spring was deciding to show its face. The shop was quiet and quaint with the sound of dishes barely tapping each other. You can hear the end of autumn air each time someone would go in and out of the door. I would look upon the entrance on occasion, from sipping my beverage to see if Denise had arrived. My nerves were on edge, and I didn't know if I was going to realize how pitiful she was and take the high road or order another cup of hot coffee just to throw it in her face.

I took another sip of coffee while my leg was jackhammering the floor as it went up and down, showing how impatient I was getting. I was able to take a deep breath as another gush of wind came in.

"Marissa?"

I used this unique meditation technique to calm myself, I opened my eyes, and there she stood. The perfect figure, the ideal height; she plainly passed the paper bag test. Looks alone, I can understand why Nathan was attracted. I became a little uneasy at that acknowledgment.

"Denise?"
I stood so I would be ready for anything. I am not sure how involved Denise and Nathan were. Reluctantly, I stretched out my hand to shake hers, not knowing what to expect. Not surprisingly, but she was quite pleasant for someone who is a mistress.

"Hi, sorry I'm running a little late. It's been one of those mornings."

"Oh, I understand." Her independent nature made me realize how caged I had been.

She brought live, adventurous energy. The type of energy you need to be free, free to explore who you genuinely are unapologetic, with no regret or fear holding you back. I became jealous.
Denise seemed to be what I never dared to be, and that is someone who depends and puts her confidence in herself and not a relationship. I chose love and will always, but at the expense of possible unhappiness, is the chance even worth it?

We both sat down across from each other, and there was a quick but awkward silence. It was the type of stillness where you both have so much to say, but you're not sure who should go first.

"So."

I figured I would begin since I did make the initial call to set up this showdown.

"So." She replied. I wasn't sure what would be the next thing out of our mouths. I took a deep breath, and she said. "I guess I'm able to sit here now."

I chuckled a little.

From what I remember, she always had a smart mouth. She was rather quiet at first but branched out more socially in junior high. It was the opposite for me. The day after my body was violated by Lewis's presumptuous, ego-driven, perverted existence, I could not bear to look at myself in the mirror. The shame that came over me seemed to be unbearable. But as usual, I took that hurt and hid it on the inside. I pretended to get by and moved forward on in relationships and life as if nothing ever happened.

Nevertheless, I could feel the world closing in on me faster these days. My past was creating a burden on me, and I was ready to fall in love. I knew David was a strong man, but I would not want him to carry my load as well.

"Touché."

By the look on both of our faces, we both went back to where seating arrangements dictated your status. Our smudge smirks were understood. The circumstances were uncomfortable to be in for both of us.

"Look, Marissa. I don't know what to say other than I'm sorry things happened the way they did, on my part."
She seemed sincere, and all I wanted to do was to choke this bitch, but I was still curious to know about these "things" that happened.

"Look, Denise, I understand that you and Nate had a history, and I'm sure if you had stayed with him back then, he probably…"

"Wait. If I had stayed?" She had this grin that annoyed me. This was not a laughing matter, especially after she decided to break up my home.

"Yes, stayed."

"I'm not sure what Nathan had told you, but we were young and unaware of what we both wanted. It's just that now, I guess, growing up and being more knowledgeable of what love really is…"

"And what do you know about love?" No, she didn't. Was she about to tell me that she and Nate called themselves being in love? "What can you possibly know? First, love would have not led you to screw another woman's husband, my dear."

"Okay, there is no need to get your panties all up in a bunch. I never slept with Nate." She proclaimed, but I did not believe it one bit.

"Whatever you say, Denise, I just wanted to let you know that even though I am not very fond of you by no means, I don't wish any ill will against you. And trust, you would not be the main reason why Nate and I are no longer husband and wife. It is more to it than that, but I wouldn't expect you to understand that."

"Oh trust," She said sarcastically as to throw my words back at me, "I'm aware that it was more to it than that."

She began to gather her things. It was for the best.

"You know what Marissa, for someone who is so in tune with "what love is," why are you so pressed about someone who clearly didn't show you that or didn't care enough to let you know how they really felt about you. Instead, they shared that with someone else. You're sad."

It took everything in me to keep from jumping across the booth and smacking her across her face, but instead, I decided to take her words and give them some thought. Why was I so interested in knowing? It was clear that love was not amid our marriage from the beginning. He only settled for me because he couldn't have her, and I think she knew that. Her attitude was showing that she felt she had the advantage, but little did she know Nathan was not only sweet, but he could be just as sour.

"You're right, Denise. I admit, I may not be that knowledgeable about love as you are. But I do know this I have enough love for myself to at least respect its power and what it can do. So, I hope what you think you have now is true."
She got up from the booth we were in and smacked her teeth. I can tell she was annoyed by my comment, it seemed to hit home. It looks like she wasn't too confident about her feelings of Nathan either.

"You have a nice day, Marissa." I gave a slight grin to show how unbothered I was about her jab at my intelligence.

She started to walk away but turned back, "Oh, and say hello to little Nate for me." She gave me a phony smile before walking away.

I was furious.

CHAPTER 33

The conversation I had with Denise the day after lingered in my head. I drove over to my fathers' home for a visit since he had been feeling a little under the weather for the past few months, and I wanted to make sure he had everything he needed. He was quite different from what I remembered in my childhood. I guess old age and reflection can give you a reality check which brings about change.

Denise's request of me to tell my son "hello" plucked within my spirit all night. I couldn't get it off my mind. My curiosity-built day by day. What a low blow to let me know that she had been spending time with my son without my knowledge.

"Bitch!"

I wanted to get to the bottom of that, but for now, my father was more important than Denise's amateur attempts to get under my skin.

I turned the corner, heading toward my fathers' house. My heart dropped to my feet. I could not put the car in park fast enough before opening the car door and running toward the house.

"DAD!!"

The ambulance was blocking the driveway, and the front door was wide open. With every step and breath, time appeared to cease. I was dreading the inevitable. I stepped over the threshold and entered the house. I could see the stretcher in the living room area from the door, my father's feet were visible, but a white blanket covered most of his body.

My heart began to pound, and the tears started to welp up in the corner of my eyes. When it rains, it pours. I slowly approached where my father was with paramedics everywhere. I trembled at the thought of experiencing, which could be the worst day any child could go thru. I passed the dining area, where I spent many nights listening to my mother and father argue over frivolous things.

"Marissa?"
I looked to my left, and there he was. Beautiful as ever, and for a quick moment, he took my mind off the tragedy at hand. He stopped me dead in my tracks.

"James?" I said, holding back tears. "What are you doing here?"

He stood, and his statue was much taller than I remembered. He had a look of much concern on his face.

"I'm so sorry, Marissa." I wondered what he was doing here, but that had to wait. I had to get to my Dad.

Now, I must pause and write that while editing, I had a revelation. You know those times in your life, right when you think it may be over, God allows a sign in many ways? If we choose the unjust route, and vice versa, it will turn out for OUR good.

[CONTINUE]

I slowly approached the living room, praying that my father was alright. Even though we had our disagreements with each other over the years, he was still my Dad; the only father I knew and believe it or not, I needed him in my life. One of the paramedics began to approach me, I began to shake. I was afraid of what he was about to tell me, but I swallowed hard and took a deep breath to soothe my nerves.

"Hello, are you another family member of the patient?"

"Yes," I responded softly.

"Okay, come with me. I need to know more medical history if you're able to provide it?" He gestured for me to follow him to where my father laid on the stretcher.

"Baby girl." I heard my father's weak voice, and a sense of relief came upon me. I began to cry and leaned over and hugged him tightly.

"I'm alright baby girl, don't cry."

He rubbed my back to comfort me. I never have known my father to be tender. Here is this man stretched out in the middle of his home, probably close to death, and he decides to comfort me instead when I should be strengthening him.

"Dad, what's going on, what happened?" I looked up at the paramedic for answers and back at my father. "What is James doing here?" I looked back toward the dining area. James was now standing in the middle of the hallway that led to the living room. His hands in his pocket and head down, pacing a little as if he were more upset than I was about my father. It was strange.

"Well, your father has cancer as far as we know, and we were called out because he had collapsed."
"Collapsed?" I repeated. "Cancer?" I was so confused. "Dad, what is going on and tell me now."

"Darling." My father began to say but was interrupted by the paramedic.

"We have to get him to the hospital now, he has to get checked out. You can follow us there." the paramedic insisted.

"Okay, yeah, sure." I collected myself and allowed the medical personnel to do their job. I stood there watching every movement making sure my father was handled with the care I would give him. I followed behind them as they took him out to the cruiser to transport him. James was already outside, rubbing the top of his head and nervous. I still had my keys in hand and stood on the porch as they placed my father in the ambulance. I looked over at James.

"You alright? What happened, James?"

James looks at me with bloodshot eyes. It looked like he had been crying for days. I reached out to touch him, but he stepped back. Why, I wasn't sure, but it was not like him. "I think I'm going to throw up." He went back into the house.

I was so confused about his behavior, but I could not be concerned with that right now. I headed toward my car and got in as quickly as possible. The ambulance started to pull out of the driveway, and I proceeded to follow it down the road. We made the right that would take us to the expressway to the hospital just a few miles away. I could not believe my father had cancer this whole time and did not tell me. I began to be upset but also relieved that he hadn't passed away.

As I followed behind the ambulance, I wondered why James was acting so weird. We have been living next door to each other for practically all our lives, and our families had gotten close. Maybe he had come by for a visit, and that's how he found father. Finding out about father having cancer, upset me. He could have told me the entire truth on why he insisted I move back. I'm not sure what was wrong, but something was unsettling to me. I needed answers.

CHAPTER 34

It was almost dusk by the time my Dad arrived and was placed in a room for observation. The beep of the heart monitor attached to him started to create a musical rhythm in my head. It kept me in a trance while I stared at my father hopelessly. Thoughts of what was to become of my father's health weighed heavily on me. He was sound asleep, exhausted from all the nurses coming in and out, poking him at every chance they got.

Over at the side of the bed, there was a telephone. I decided to call David again to check on little Nathan to make sure he had eaten dinner and gotten ready for bed. Having him in my life right now was right on time. God sure has a way of showing up when you need him.

"Hey, I know I'm a bother?"

"No, no, not at all. How's everything going? Do you need me to bring anything or...?" David was very considerate and knew how to make me feel at peace in the most disruptive situation.

"Oh, no. Dad's asleep right now, so when his tests come back, I'll make it home to gather a few things. For now, I'm okay." I didn't tell David about how strange James was at the house before coming here. "How's Junior, did he eat all his dinner?"

"Yeah, he did. I ordered some takeout; we played a few video games; now he is settled in for bed. He's alright, don't worry about anything."

"Did he remember to brush his teeth?"

"Yes, mommy. Don't worry," he teased.

It was the first time I laughed or smiled all day. Father began to awaken from his nap. I can see his legs move under the covers, trying to adjust to get more comfortable.

"Alright, it looks like he's waking up now." I took a deep breath of relief. "I'll talk to you later. Kiss my baby for me." I started to tear up a bit. The weight of the day finally settled in, and the pressure began to rise. What was really going on? I gripped the phone with both hands, hoping that my love was felt thru the airways back home. "Oh, and David?"

"Yeah?"

"I love you, and thanks again."

The line was silent for a quick moment. This was my first-time telling David that I loved him. I am sure on the other end; he probably was trying to process the emotion just as I was. It did feel good to finally say it out loud, to release what had been in my heart for some time now. The silver lining had finally been drawn. I felt rejuvenated and ready to take on any other adversity that may have showed its wicked head.

"Love you more."

My heart was full, and instead of doubting those words being said to me like I've done so many times in the past, I believed him, wholeheartedly, and nothing and no one could have told me any different that this love wasn't real.

CHAPTER 35

"Mr. Orville, it looks like your vitals have stabilized, but I still want to keep you overnight for observation. You took a pretty hard fall, and given your current health condition and age, you can never be too cautious."

The doctor came with my father's test results, and everything seemed fine. I was grateful and relieved to hear this, so an extra day in the hospital to make sure he was well enough would not hurt. But I knew Dad, his stubbornness will kick in and make things difficult for all of us.

"I feel fine, I just needed to rest. There is no need for me to be here. Tell 'em, Marissa."

"Dad, I think you should take the advice of the doctor; just stay the night. I'll be here with you." I grabbed my father's hand to try and comfort him.

I knew he hated hospitals of any kind, especially being in and out of them when he and mom were together. "He'll be alright, doctor. Thank you so much."

"Oh no, I understand." He had a sweet smile and bedside manner. "I assure you, Mr. Orville, there will be no more poking on you tonight." He chuckled a bit. "Alright, if everything stays the same, I will see you in the morning and see about getting you discharge."

My Dad shook his head slightly and reluctantly agreed. We were left with our thoughts as the doctors and nurse exited the room. I was relieved that my father would be fine, but I still wondered what had occurred before I arrived at the house. I gazed upon my father's face as he took a deep breath. He gave a slight grin as if he knew there was more that needed to be said but didn't know where to begin. I decided to relieve him of that thought and addressed the elephant in the room.

"Why didn't you tell me you were sick?"

He took a deep breath, already aggravated by the questioning of his decision not to tell me, "Why do you think, Marissa? I did not want you to worry about me. I have it under control."

"Oh. I see."

"Alright now. Don't get your panties all in a bunch."

I always had an impulse to be a little sassy at times, but I believe this time was warranted. "Well, how do you expect me to feel, and why was James at the house? He was acting strange. Did he do something to you?"

"What?" he laughed at the thought. "No." He seemed very hesitant. He sat up in the bed a little. With sincere eyes he stretched out his hand and asked, "Pass me a little water, dear. I'm a little thirsty."

I walked over to the cart where the water pitcher was and poured him a cup. The water was chilled but not cold. I wrapped a paper towel around it so he could have it just in case he spilled some. He drank the water as if he had not had anything to drink in a long time. I think he was passing the time to keep from telling me the truth.

"Well, Dad."

He took a deep breath as he gave the cup back to me. "I saw James as he was coming to visit his parents, that's all. I was on the porch. I waved, and he stopped to chit-chat."

There was more to it than that, I was sure of it. "About?"

"Marissa, some things are hard to explain or just…" He appeared to be getting weak. He leaned back a little, breathing heavier.

"Are you okay? You need the nurse?" I placed my hand on his forehead. He didn't feel warm, but something was bothering him. "Well, I'm sure he's still at his parents."

I'll *just ask him when I go back to get you some clothes.* I thought.

"NO, MARISSA!" My Dad was so loud I thought the whole hospital heard him.

"WHAT? Dad, what's going on?" He would not say anything, just shake his head.

I questioned him more and more, and the more I asked, I can see his aggravation until he just blurted it out.

"HE'S YOUR BROTHER DAMMIT!" my father covered his face in shame and began to sob.

CHAPTER 36

She was to blame for every adversity and hardship. My tormented life was brought on by me living within another's sinful acts that had nothing to do with me. I was cursed. I was cursed like Canaan was because of his father Ham's transgression. I left the hospital to head home to pick up a fresh pair of clothes. My mind was racing, trying to process what I was told by my father. I could not believe what I had heard. My father, with tears in his eyes, began to reveal to me the unthinkable.

"He's your brother."

I couldn't get those words out of my head. I had committed incest due to my mother's lies. My father began to tell me how she and Mr. Deitrick had an affair, and she ended up pregnant. She said it was rape, but my father knew better. I do remember the awkwardness that was thick enough to cut with a knife the day we ran into the Deitrick's in the grocery store one Sunday afternoon:

"Hey, how are you doing?" James's Dad waved to us as we approached the bakery area where they were.

Everyone exchanged greetings but my mother. She seemed a little nervous. She tried to hide it, but I saw that something was off. I was hoping she was not having another one of her episodes.

"James!" said Mrs. Deitrick with her small stature and pixy haircut.

I thought she was very graceful, dainty. James was staring so hard at me; he didn't hear his mother call his name.

"Hello," I said and stuck out my hand for him to shake. His palms were sweaty and clammy.

His Dad laughed and looked at my mother, who was avoiding eye contact. "Teenage boys."

They all laughed a little as if they were the only ones with the secret, and no one else knew.

I finally made it home and began to pack some items. I wanted to be incredibly quiet as to not wake up, David. He was sound to sleep. The house was clean, and Junior was in his room, resting like a baby. After checking on him and putting everything in the car, I sat in the drivers' seat with my hand on the steering wheel in a gaze. I began to feel squeamish. I opened the car door and walked a couple of feet and threw up from the thought of James and me together. I was disgusted.

How could no one tell me? Hate began to grow within me, and I had to let it out somehow. I went back into the house to clean up a little, and I headed back out. I started down the road, and instead of heading back to the hospital, I began to take the route to my mothers' home. The closer I got, the more furious I began to feel. It was in the middle of the night, and I did not care.

I finally made it and sat in front of her house for a while. I wanted an explanation. I deserved an answer; after all, this was her fault. Once I calmed down to the point where I felt I wouldn't strangle my mother, I got out of the car and walked to the front door. The pathway to the door seemed endless as I slowly walked toward it and knocked. I knocked once more after a few minutes passed, and the porch light came on.

I saw her peek thru the curtains. I would usually smile and wave to let her know it was me, but all I could do was give her a stern glare. The look on her face was of concern. She did not know what she would be facing once she opened the door. As the door opened, my heart began to pound. I looked upon my mother's face, and tears began to form.

"Oh, darling. What's the matter?" she said.

I could not take it anymore; I began to tremble at the reality of my life. "Why, mom? WHY?"

She looked at me up and down and reached out for me. I stepped back so she would not touch me. "What's the matter, Marissa?" she stepped outside and looked both ways to try and figure out what was going on.

"Why, mom, how could you do this?"

"Marissa. Calm down, honey. Tell me what's the matter." She seemed so sincere.

"YOU!" I did not realize it until I saw her look down, but I began to form a fist. I was so furious. She looked back up at me and took a step back. Her face changed from an innocent one to no expression at all.

"Would you like to come in?" she looked evil.

"No, I wouldn't. Why must I suffer over and over from your transgression, huh? Why?"

"Oh, Marissa! Don't be so dramatic."

"I SLEPT WITH MY BROTHER BECAUSE OF YOU. MY BROTHER DAMMIT!" I was screaming at the top of my lungs. How dare she be so nonchalant about it. I started to feel rage creep back into my whole being.

[SLAP]

My hand stung from the impact of my hand against my mothers' face. She almost fell back but grabbed the side of the rail on her porch. She touched her cheek and looked at me with the coldest eyes I've ever seen.

"You think you're better than me, huh? Who are you to think that you can go thru life, and everything will be just peachy? Well, honey, wake up, it ain't like that." She began to turn and walk toward her door to open it. She stopped and turned around. "If you weren't such a whore and hadn't been sleeping around, you would have never put yourself in this situation."

I could not believe the words that were coming out of her mouth. She was genuinely delusional and did not care about her actions. Yes, I did sleep with James out of my own desire, but I would have never loved him or looked at him in that way if I had known the truth. She was not going to manipulate her way out of her responsibility as a mother to me anymore.

"You're sick. I want you to stay out of my life and out of my child's life. You're dead to me. I pray God has mercy on your soul because you have none from me."

"Well, that's splendid. Typical Marissa, thinking it's all about her."

"I learn from the best."

I walked back to my car and left her standing on her doorstep. I had to release the demons that haunted my mother for years. I refused to allow them to penetrate my life anymore. I did not have a choice on who birth me, but I do have an opportunity to choose who I allow in my life. I, for once, wanted to do what was best for me, and cutting ties with the toxic relationship with my mother was the step I needed to take.

For me, being happy is a personal thing, it has nothing to do with anyone else.

CHAPTER 37

It was almost dawn by the time I made it back to the hospital. Dad was sound asleep, he looked peaceful. I went over and placed my hand on his forehead as I prayed for him. I closed my eyes, and the memories of him made my past feelings seemed to die. I had a conclusion now of who he was and what life had forced him to become. He could have easily discarded me by the wayside, to forget about me, it would have made his life more comfortable. But, instead, he decided to care for a child that was born out of iniquity. He chose to love me the best way he knew how with the given circumstances.

I wept.

I sat back on the small couch that was in his room and just stared at him while he slept. My mind starting to go over and over the memories of what had happened in my past. I sorted thru each one to arrive at a better understanding, to see the big picture. The last words I said to my mom was not of my character. I was a forgiving person, but she had a trend of pushing the buttons that I hated I possessed, yet I meant every word.

I started to pray for forgiveness as I wept and released all the negativity that was guarding my life. All I wanted was to be loved. I wanted to love. Maybe she was right, I did live in a fantasy that love would be easy. Why shouldn't it be? Something so divine and perfect should not be that hard to obtain. Regardless, I'm willing to take risks, and that involves clearing the path so it may manifest.

CHAPTER 38

I felt a presence in the room as I was touched by the sun coming from the hospital room window. I fell asleep on the small couch after the long night I had. Even though I had gone thru a very emotional circumstance the day before, I felt free and ready to journey down a path of righteousness and affirmation. I slowly turned to see my father was awake and looking well. I sat up and could not believe my eyes.

"Morning." His face looked much different now. My feelings were unsure, and I wasn't sure how I would react once I saw him again, but I was glad he was here. James had come by to visit to make sure my father was alright.

"Hi!" It was an awkward silence. I could tell he already knew that I was aware of who he was.

"Don't be afraid, sweetie." My dad emphasized. "He told me everything, it's not your fault."

I took a deep breath. I looked over at James, standing at the end of my fathers' bed. I wanted him to say something, but what could he say. He looked down at his feet as he began to try and put into words what he was feeling.

"Marissa, I'm so sorry. I know over the years growing up, I did not do right by you. I just could not understand what the hesitation was. Knowing what we know, it all makes sense now. Please forgive me. I didn't know, same as you, and I hope we can try and figure out how we can process and deal with this together." He began to choke up.

I'm sure he was just as confused as I was. I stood and walked over to James. I held out both arms to welcome him into an embrace. I have hugged James many times in the past, but this was the best one yet. It felt warm, sincere, and I could feel that he cared. It will take some time to get past this, but with the help of God, I believe we did have a chance of coming out of this trial brand new.

CHAPTER 39

"Thank God!" Dad was ecstatic to be home and in his own bed.

"Oh, it wasn't that bad old man."

"Shhiii, yeah, it was. I hate hospitals. I'm so glad to be back home."

"Well, I hope you know that I'm going to be on you like white on rice about your health now. I'm still not over you, not telling me about having cancer. But we'll leave that for another day.

"Yeah, yeah, I know." He rolled his eyes as he got in the bed to rest. I gave him his medicine and made sure he was comfortable.

"I got to get back home and check on Junior. He's probably running David rugged by now." I giggled a little at the thought of those two. David had been perfect thru this whole ordeal. If I did not have him to keep me sane, I would not know what to do.

"Yeah, he is." He said, laughing. "That David fellow?"

"What about him?" I was folding some clothes that were in a basket in the corner.

"Well, he seems to really care about you, maybe even love you."

I looked at my father and smiled a little. It did feel good to hear that coming from him. If someone like my father recognized David's treatment of me in the same light that I did, maybe I was on the right path. It was refreshing to hear.

"Maybe so, let's see what happens, nosey." I kissed him on the forehead and covered him with his blanket. "There's a plate in the refrigerator of chicken and rice if you get hungry and some other snacks as well. Be sure to drink your water too, dad, no funny business." I placed my hand on my hips as an indicator that I meant what I said.

"Alright, why do kids become your parents when you get old, I will never know."

"Bye, Daddy!" I headed out the door to go home and realized I was beginning to enjoy our relationship. Now, more than I have in the past. I would have never thought that we would become this close. The mystery of life can be sneaky, and you can never be prepared for its revelation.

David was in the backyard playing with Nathan Jr. when I finally made it home. I stood in the doorway and watch them from afar. Nathan loved David, and it was all over his face. His smile was as bright as the sun that was shining upon them from above. I wasn't sure where each ray of light began or ended. He was happy, I was happy, genuinely happy. I began to smile, and I knew everything was going to be okay. David caught a glimpse of me at the door and waved. He guided Junior toward me, and as he began to run with excitement, I dreamt of this very moment happening every day of my life. I deserved it, and so did he.

"Slow down, little man." David's smile filled me with so much joy. I felt blessed. "Hey." he kissed me, and I melted.

"Hey."

"You alright?"

"Yeah, sure." I hugged Nate and kissed the top of his head.

"Hi, Mommy." He ran past me into the kitchen and grabbed the bottle of water that I always leave for him.

David embraced the right side of my face and looked into my eyes. "What's on your mind? Somethings wrong."

"No, not anymore. Well, it's a long story." I began to chuckle at the thought of what happened over the past two to three days.

"Okay, well, tell me about it."

"Later. Let's get ready for dinner."

"Alright."

I finally got dinner ready, and we sat down to eat. We laughed and talked, and it was the perfect evening. I called my father to check on him again, and he was doing fine. He was watching one of the old western cowboys shows he loved. Nathan Jr. was sound to sleep after getting ready for bed, and David and I were comfortable on the couch with a glass a wine. I felt like silk in his arms, and no one could tell me any different, that I was where I needed to be.

"I found out something horrific day before yesterday." I began.

David set up a little to brace himself for what I was about to say. "What?"

I began telling him about James and about him being my sibling, how I denounced my mother's presence in my life, his face was in awe as if he could not believe what he was hearing.

"David, I'm messed up. I'm not sure if I would be a good fit for you or what will happen in the future. I do love you, but I couldn't imagine you going thru life dealing with my emotional state unless I get some sort of counseling for all of this."

"We all have a past; we all have issues, Marissa. How we deal with them is the catch, going forward. You can't tell me how to love you. My full concentration is on you, and I hope yours is on me. There are things you cannot control in your life, and there is nothing you can do about it, but love has no condition. Perfection does not need love, imperfection does. So, since were two imperfect people who know how to love, how about we do that together."

Tears started to fall, as I have never heard anything purer. I could not deny it. I was caught up and never wanted to come down.

"I love you, David."

He wrapped his arms around me and kissed me gently. My face was held in his hands, so

I may gaze upon his face. With a deep breath, he looked into my eyes.

"Marry me, Marissa."

CHAPTER 40

Sometimes finding our way derives from us losing it in the first place. I have longed for this day my whole life. The day that I would be free, free to love unconditionally without any strings attached. I thought I had found love in James but turned out he was a test to see how strong I was to see what I was made of. I thought Nathan was the love of my life, but he taught me to not be afraid to take a chance. He taught me to jump at the chance at true love, even if it did hurt a little bit.

It was impossible to love my father, but instead, he taught me that love has no expectations; it just is. I did not know love had come into my life, but it revealed itself when I needed it most. David was that example of the type of love I needed. The more I was with him, the more I began to love myself. He allowed me to be who I was, faults, and all. My forever had finally come, and I was ready. I looked in the mirror and took a deep breath as my father walked into the room.

"Last chance, sweetie, you're sure?"

I smiled at my father thru the mirror, and he smiled back at me. "I haven't been so sure of anything in my life. Today, I'm free of any doubt for the first time."

He walked over to me and helped me to my feet. He looked at me, and a sense pride was on his face. "You have grown to be more than I could have imagined, I'm so proud of you, Marissa." I hugged my father as tight as I could. My heart was so full, and the rapture I was caught up in I never wanted to come down from.

"Love you, daddy, and thank you."

The Apostle Paul preached to the Corinthians that love is patient and kind. It does not envy, nor boast and never proud. Love is honorable and unselfish. Love forgives and does not delight in evil but rejoices with the truth. Love protects, always trusts, always hopes, always perseveres. If you believe in love, it will never fail you.

It was a joyous occasion, and I could not wait to see David standing at the altar. Walking out of that room was like entering a whole new life, and I was ready for anything that came my way.

EPILOGUE

LEAH

In and out of foster homes was my life for as long as I could remember. My life, well, it was not a picnic for sure. I am sure others have their own story of ups and downs and tribulations, but this was mine, and I am mad as hell. It wasn't fair. Why couldn't I have the perfect life that I see on television day in and day out? Why couldn't I have a mom that cared about me more than she cared about her crack habit? Why couldn't I have a dad that was more than just a sperm donor? Sometimes I had thoughts of suicide because what was the point. If I couldn't live in a world that surrounded me with love, there was no need to be alive. There was no need to exist. That is what I was doing, existing.

My thoughts raced thru my head as I traveled to now my fourth or fifth foster home. I looked at the rear-view mirror from the back seat and caught a glance of Miss Shannon looking. I rolled my eyes not because I was angry, but I knew she cared more than the other caseworkers I had had. It was not her fault, I wasn't mad at her, it was just my way of not letting my guard down, a form of protection.

I always had to protect myself. God knows there was no one else in my corner, and for this reason, I had to turn to stone. My head began to hurt as it always did ever since I was five years old. I touched the spot at the top of my head, where I felt the throbbing and placed my head in my hand and leaned against the car door. As I closed my eyes to try and numb the pain, my dreams, rather nightmares went back to one of the worst foster homes I had been in:

"AHH!" I yelled. I fell to the floor and started to crawl toward the kitchen, screaming. "Madea, Madea!"

Madea was an elderly black woman in her sixties, I believe. She was a caterer, and we would help her from time to time with the affairs of her business. She had a grandson living with her that was evil and vile as they came. He was the reason for my headaches. I could not stand him, and he knew it, but I was afraid of him. I was just a little girl; what could I possibly do. Madea never believes anything we tell her about him.

Blood started to run down my back and dripped on the floor. I was hysterical and thought I was going to die. The last thing I saw was Madea hovering over me, looking confused.

"Oh My God! What happened, Darrius?"

I slowly felt myself drifting off as my eyes closed in her arms.